# Surf, Sand and Skeletons

Sapphire Beach Cozy Mystery Series
(Book 2)

## Angela K. Ryan

John Paul Publishing

TEWKSBURY, MASSACHUSETTS

Angela K. Ryan
John Paul Publishing
Post Office Box 283
Tewksbury, MA 01876

Publisher's Note: This is a work of fiction. Names, characters, places, and incidents are a product of the author's imagination. Locales and public names are sometimes used for atmospheric purposes. Any resemblance to actual people, living or dead, or to businesses, companies, events, institutions, or locales is completely coincidental.

Cover Design © 2019 MariahSinclair.com
Book Layout © 2017 BookDesignTemplates.com

Surf, Sand and Skeletons/ Angela K. Ryan. -- 1st ed.
ISBN: 978-0-9981575-8-0

# A Note of Thanks from the Author

I would like to warmly thank all those who generously shared their time and knowledge in the research of this book, especially:

Jacki Strategos, Premier Sotheby's
International Realty, Marco Island

Carol Buccieri
Bella Stella Beads, Haverhill, Massachusetts

Marco Island Fire Rescue
Marco Island, Florida

Any errors are my own.

# Chapter 1

WITH THROBBING FEET and sore arms, Connie Petretta plopped down onto a metal folding chair to give her aching body a rest from scrubbing clean every inch of the eight-hundred-square-foot shop that would soon be the home of *Just Jewelry*, her handmade jewelry business. She was exhausted, but the satisfaction she felt from the hard work was reminiscent of the long days she spent volunteering in Africa after college. Like then, the job was tiresome, but her passion for the work carried her through.

That, and the knowledge that in a few short hours she would be spending the evening overlooking the Gulf of Mexico with friends in the beachfront condo she had recently inherited from her aunt and namesake Concetta Belmonte.

Since her return to Sapphire Beach a few days before, Connie had been counting down the minutes to when she could catch up with her cherished friends. It had only been three months since they were last all together, but it seemed like a year.

Relocating from Boston to southwest Florida was a bold move, but she couldn't wait to begin living her new dream of selling Fair Trade jewelry and her own handmade pieces to the residents and tourists who flocked to picturesque downtown Sapphire Beach. She had the urge to pinch herself to be sure she wasn't dreaming, but her weary body assured her she was well-grounded in reality.

"I think I'll join you, honey," Grace Jenkins, her only employee and one of the friends who would be coming to dinner, called from across the shop. Grace had been Concetta's best and most loyal friend, never leaving her side during her brief battle with cancer.

Connie pulled open another metal folding chair for Grace before going out back for a couple of glasses of iced tea. She was glad she thought to have a refrigerator delivered first thing upon her arrival.

"Grace, you have been here well beyond the twenty hours per week I'm paying you for," Connie said, handing her a glass and easing back into the chair.

Grace held up her palm to Connie and turned her face away. "You know how much I believe in this store," she said. "I wouldn't dream of being anywhere else."

The caffeine in the black tea, which she had brewed extra strong that morning, knowing it would be a long day, was kicking in nicely. Connie put her empty glass on the floor and retrieved her laptop from the circular counter in the middle of the store, which would soon serve as the checkout area.

She opened the flyer she had been working on for the grand opening and felt a surge of excitement, which magnified her caffeine boost. She couldn't wait to show off her shop to the Sapphire Beach community.

"I scheduled the grand opening for the first Saturday in April, a couple of weeks before The Great Lexodus," Connie said, the expression causing a smirk to push its way onto her lips. The Great Lexodus, as Aunt Concetta had explained one time, was when the snowbirds headed north, many in their luxury cars, to return home in time for Easter and to escape the brutally hot summer months in subtropical Florida. "That will give me the slower summer months to restock inventory in time for their return."

After all the packing and unpacking, Connie was looking forward to spending those hot and humid summer days creating jewelry in the comfort of the air-conditioned shop. But for now, her focus was on the grand opening and all the preparations that had to take place in the two weeks and three days between now and then.

In addition to getting the physical store set up and all the advertising that had to happen, there was her website to think about, online venues, and photos for social media. With so many tasks swirling around in her mind like an ocean whirlpool, she constantly had the feeling she was forgetting something.

The sound of the door chime pulled them from their conversation. It was her contractor, Steve, a dark-haired man wearing jeans and a white polo shirt. With him was a woman who appeared to be in her early thirties, her shoulder-length blond hair tied back with a lime-green bandanna. Connie had hired

Steve to oversee the renovations while she was back in Boston selling her condo and training her successor at *Feeding the Hungry*, the non-profit where she had worked for the past twelve years.

Connie stood to greet him. "Everything looks fabulous, Steve."

"I know we've talked extensively over the phone," he said, "but I wanted to stop by now that you're back in town to be sure you were happy with the work and to introduce you to one of my carpenters, Brittany. She's been working on another job, but she'll be helping me knock off the final punch list."

"It's great to meet you," Connie said, shaking Brittany's hand. "I'm thrilled to be working with a female carpenter. You don't see that often enough."

Brittany smiled warmly. "A good friend and mentor helped me to see that I am capable of accomplishing anything I set my mind to."

Steve took a quick walk around the store. "I can't believe you got this place cleaned so quickly. I thought you'd want to hire someone to take care of that."

"Absolutely not," Grace interjected, putting an arm around Connie's shoulders. "There's no need to pay for something we can do ourselves."

Connie was pleased with the finishes she had chosen. The fresh coat of baby-blue paint against the driftwood accent wall gave the interior of the store a beachy vibe, while the hardwood floors, freshly sanded and stained, still held some of the nicks and scratches from years of wear and tear. Connie had elected not to replace them because of the history and character they contained. And the brushed gold and crystal chandelier above the circular checkout counter added a touch of elegance. Connie had dubbed the style 'beachy-glam.'

Of course, any remodel, beachy-glam or otherwise, was expensive. Fortunately, she had the money from the sale of her condo back in Boston to get her started, while she got everything off the ground. And she would be eternally grateful to her aunt for leaving her the beachfront condo mortgage-free.

"You did an amazing job, Steve. Every time I look at those empty shelves, I feel like a child on

Christmas morning. I can't wait to stock them with jewelry and for the furniture to arrive tomorrow."

"There's just a small punch list left," Steve said. "Brittany or I will be in before the end of the week to complete it. Just be careful. There are a couple of loose floorboards out back in the storage area," he said as they were leaving.

By the time Connie and Grace finished cleaning the last few spots, not even the afternoon sun streaming through the windows could find a speck of dirt. They gave each other a tired high-five and decided to call it a day.

Connie stayed behind to snap a few pictures for her social media pages that showed the store's progress to her growing number of followers.

"I'm going to head out, honey, and take a hot bath before dinner tonight," Grace said. "What can I bring?"

"Nothing. Everything is taken care of. Just come."

After Grace left, Connie wandered out back to the storage room to look through some of her inventory. Metal shelving wrapped around the ten-by-ten room, where, in addition to product, she stored beads, pliers, tweezers, and other jewelry-making tools and supplies.

In addition to showcasing her talent for making stunning jewelry, a skill that Connie learned while volunteering and living in Kenya after college, *Just Jewelry* would also provide much-needed work for women in developing countries through the Fair Trade portion of the store. It was the perfect way to combine her love of jewelry-making with her passion for humanitarian work.

In choosing artisans to supply her jewelry, Connie had started with the communities in Africa where she already had connections. Her former boss, Sam O'Neil, also connected her with some of his associates in South America, where he had spent a year before leaving a successful corporate career to found *Feeding the Hungry*. The boxes of bracelets, necklaces, and earrings had arrived safely by way of Grace's apartment and sat tucked away and unopened in the storeroom.

In addition, between everything else taking place back home in Boston, Connie had been hard at work every spare moment creating jewelry over the past few months and shipping items that she had already made. Some of the more intricate necklaces had taken her more than thirty hours to create, while other smaller pieces, such as earrings, had taken less than an hour. It was no small feat getting the store stocked and ready for the grand opening. Fortunately, the initial rush wouldn't last too long, and she would have the summer to restock, hopefully with a better sense of what sells in Sapphire Beach.

As she looked at the boxes, Connie couldn't contain herself. She just had to open at least one or two. She got a key from her purse and cut through the packing tape on one of the boxes from Kenya. Hidden among the one-of-a-kind necklaces, earrings, and bracelets was a note from her longtime friend, Dura, whom she had met while serving in Kenya. Dura was her own age, thirty-four, and was the first person to teach her how to make jewelry. She was also instrumental in identifying local artisans for Connie's new venture. Warmth spread through Connie's chest as she read Dura's note: *Praying for you and your important venture, my friend.*

The second box was filled with a colorful array of jewelry from Ecuador. The blue, green, yellow, and orange hues took her breath away. They would be a perfect alternative to the earthier tones of the Kenyan jewelry. Connie carefully rewrapped them until she could properly display them on her shelves, and after a few minutes of further exploration, she put back the boxes and forced herself to leave. She still had dinner to prepare for company that evening. There would be plenty of time to admire each piece as she stocked the shelves.

On her way out, Connie absentmindedly stepped on one of the loose boards that Steve had warned her about, stumbling across the storeroom. *Good thing nobody was around to see that graceful move.*

When she stooped down to take a closer look, she noticed that not only were two of the wooden floorboards loose, but they also seemed to sink a little in the middle. She pulled them up and immediately saw the problem. A portion of the subfloor beneath the wooden planks had been cut out. She reached her hand into the hole and felt around. She had to reach way in, but eventually her hand hit a plastic storage box. She pulled out the box and popped open its blue cover.

She discovered a leather-bound notebook that looked like a diary, what appeared to be an old-fashioned financial ledger, and a pad of white-lined paper that contained a to-do list. She sat cross-legged on the floor to examine its contents more closely.

# Chapter 2

CONNIE PULLED OUT the financial ledger first and flipped through the dusty pages. Judging from the name, "*Natasha's Boutique*" written across the top of the first page, it looked to be the financial records of the previous shop owner. Connie knew that the shop had formerly been a women's clothing store, and Natasha Orlov, the previous owner, had disappeared without a trace less than a year ago. But beyond that, she didn't know much about Natasha or her shop. Why would Natasha keep a hard copy of her financials when everyone seemed to use computer records these days?

Putting the ledger aside, Connie pulled out the pad of white-lined paper containing a to-do list. It was dated May twelfth, but there was no year. There were only a few items on the list - pick Victoria up at 5:00 PM, reorganize the storage area, call Mickey. Mickey must refer to Mickey Miranda, the shop's landlord.

The fourth and last item on the list read, "Confront accountant with findings." What did that mean? Could that be connected to the hand-written accounting ledger? Could there be a connection between a possible confrontation with her accountant and Natasha's disappearance?

Connie took a deep breath to stop her mind from jumping ahead and reminded herself that it could all be perfectly innocent.

Lastly, Connie pulled out the diary and ran her hands across the soft, brown leather. She scanned through a few entries and quickly realized it was personal, rather than work-related. She fished her phone out of the pocket of her blue jean capris and checked the time. She had to head home shortly to prepare for company, so she wouldn't have the time to read through it all, especially since she would have to turn it over to the police.

Connie decided she had better call the police sooner rather than later. After all, if she had just discovered information that could help find Natasha, she shouldn't sit on it, not even until the next morning. But she also wanted to take a closer look. After all, she was now spending her days in the same shop Natasha had leased and would soon be in daily contact with the same people Natasha had known. Perhaps this proximity to her routine would provide her with some type of insight or perspective on Natasha's whereabouts. It couldn't hurt to at least be aware.

So, Connie snapped pictures of the to-do list and of each page of the financial ledger and journal to study them later, then placed everything back in the box.

Her first call was to her friend Elyse Miller to get some preliminary information. Elyse was the realtor who helped her get a great deal on this shop and had also quickly become a good friend. After explaining what she found, Elyse informed Connie that it was indeed last summer when Natasha went missing and that Victoria was her then-two-year-old daughter. That explained why the to-do list said to pick up Victoria at 5:00 PM.

Elyse's husband, Josh, a police detective, had taken the day off and was with Elyse. He encouraged Connie to turn in the evidence as soon as possible to his colleague, Detective Zach Hughes. He and Zach were the only two investigative officers in the Sapphire Beach Police Department, and Zach had been the lead detective on the case last summer. Josh said they had exhausted all leads and were currently working on other cases.

Connie's heart sank at the idea of calling Zach. There had been some chemistry between them just before she left Sapphire Beach a few months ago, and she didn't really want this to be the first time she saw him again - sweaty and dusty from a day of cleaning. But she pushed aside her vanity and placed the call. In about fifteen minutes, Zach was in her shop.

"Welcome back, Connie," he said with a warm smile.

"Thanks, Zach. It's great to see you. I promise to have a little reunion party for everyone once I get settled in." Tonight's get-together was just for the girls.

"How did everything go back in Boston?"

"Pretty smoothly. Thanks for the postcards." Zach had sent her a couple of different postcards depicting sea, sand, and palm trees.

"Just a little something to remind you of Sapphire Beach in case you were having second thoughts about moving here," he said with a playful smile.

"No second thoughts. I'm feeling really good about the decision." Although it had been tough leaving her parents, her sister, and her twin niece and nephew, Connie felt a deep peace surrounding her decision. This was the right next step.

Connie led Zach over to the checkout counter, where she had brought the box for easy access. "Here it is. I found it hidden beneath some loose floorboards in the storage room." Then she brought him out back to show him the spot where she discovered it. Zach pulled up the boards and reached his hand around, until he appeared satisfied that there was nothing else hiding underneath.

"I understand Natasha went missing sometime last summer."

"June of last year," Zach said, as they went back to the counter. "We conducted an investigation but weren't able to get too far. She left her two-year-old daughter with a friend, saying she just needed some time to think, and then never came back. It appears she just took off. Your landlord was furious that she skipped out on her lease."

"Did she have any reason to run away?"

"Some people suspected drugs were involved, but we didn't find any solid evidence that she was using."

Connie's heart sank at the thought of a little girl who would grow up not only without her mother, but without any answers, as well.

"I have to get back to the station, but hopefully I'll see you soon," Zach said, flashing her a smile as he left with the box.

Before going home, Connie took one last look around the shop, and a wave of excitement washed over her. She could envision exactly what it would look like this time tomorrow, after the furniture arrived. Her dream was quickly becoming a reality, and she couldn't be happier.

After locking up, Connie drove her silver Jetta back to Palm Paradise, the condominium building she now called home, and rode the elevator to the seventh floor.

Her whole body relaxed when she stepped into the exquisite condo perched above the white sandy beach and sparkling blue waters of the Gulf of Mexico. What a blessing. Her eyes still welled up whenever she thought about her aunt's generosity in leaving her the condo.

Working for a non-profit, it had taken Connie years of saving and living frugally to be able to afford the small condo outside of Boston that she had been proud to call home for the past six years. It wasn't that Connie ever had a single regret about her choice of work, but the fact remained that, without her aunt's generosity, *Just Jewelry* never would have been possible.

Ginger, her aunt's Cavalier King Charles Spaniel, whom Connie unofficially inherited along with the condo, interrupted her thoughts with an enthusiastic greeting. Connie bent down to give her four-legged friend a little love. Her heart went out to the poor little dog who had been cooped up all week while she readied the shop for furniture.

"One more day, sweet girl, and then you can start coming to work with me." Ginger looked up and wagged her tail as if she understood.

With a little time before company was due to arrive, Connie took Ginger for a walk down Sapphire Beach Boulevard, then put dinner in the oven and got ready for company.

Grace lived in the apartment next door, so she arrived first, followed by her daughter Stephanie and Elyse.

"Aunt Gertrude wanted to come, but she had already made plans," Elyse said. Gertrude was Elyse's great aunt, who also lived in Palm Paradise. "That woman has a better social life than I do."

"You and me both," Connie said, laughing. "It's so wonderful to be together again after a hectic few months." She had seen Grace and Elyse a number of times this week, but it was her first time seeing Stephanie since January.

"I love the personal touches you added to this place," Elyse said, looking around the apartment.

Connie had kept her aunt's furniture, since she had phenomenal taste, and Connie's had mainly been handed down from her parents, but she had brought and shipped many of her personal items. Connie's own pictures now decorated the walls, and beautifully carved statues, made from Kenyan wood, as well as handwoven baskets, were scattered throughout the apartment. She also brought a few plants when she drove down, in addition to purchasing others native to the tropics, lending a Floridian feel to her new home.

She even had her favorite herbs growing in pots on the balcony - basil, rosemary, parsley, and, of course, mint for her iced tea. She couldn't wait to bring the mint into the shop.

It was starting to feel more like Connie's home than her aunt's, but not so much so that she couldn't still feel Concetta at every turn. The comforting mix of old and new made her heart smile.

The women settled onto the couch with a glass of wine and a caprese salad, made with fresh basil from one of her new plants. It didn't take long to catch up on one another's lives. Then they moved to the dining table to enjoy their meal, where the conversation eventually rolled around to Natasha and her mysterious disappearance.

"How old was she?" Connie asked, slipping her hands into oven mitts and placing a pan of baked ziti on the table next to the salad. Her question wasn't addressed to anyone in particular. "Zach said that she went missing last June."

"I think she was in her late twenties," Grace said. "I met her a couple of times when I did a little shopping in her boutique. Her baby girl was with her one of the times. I remember how she doted over that little girl. It's hard to imagine she would just up and leave her behind. But I guess that goes to show that you never quite know what's going on with someone."

"Not to change the subject, but you saw Zach already?" Stephanie said, leaning forward and wearing a big smile. "What's going on there, anything worth sharing?"

Connie could tell that nothing was going to get past these women. "I did see him, but it's not what you think. I called him, because I found some objects hidden in the shop that might be connected to Natasha's disappearance." Connie described the items she found under the loose floorboards. "I didn't have a chance to go through everything, but I snapped pictures."

"I didn't hear that," Elyse said, taking another serving of pasta. Back in January, Josh had clearly expressed his feelings about anyone sticking their nose into police business. And they weren't favorable.

"You've only been back a few days, and you're already playing detective?" Grace said, shaking her head in disapproval. "Promise me you'll be careful, Connie. You almost got yourself killed looking into those murders back in January."

"I promise," Connie said, making a cross over her heart.

"By the way," Elyse said, trying to suppress a smile. "Zach's a great guy. Josh speaks highly of him, in case you're wondering."

Connie could feel her cheeks getting warm. "I'll keep that in mind."

After a wonderful evening of reconnecting with one another, her guests left. While Connie loaded the dishwasher, her mind drifted toward Natasha. When she finished cleaning, she emailed herself the photos of the items she had found and printed them out from her computer before settling onto her couch to read them.

The ledger didn't reveal much, since she had nothing to compare it to, except that, if it was correct,

Natasha's business had been bringing in a steady profit. She certainly didn't run away to escape financial problems.

Next, she looked at the diary. It took about a half-hour to skim it in its entirety, but there was one passage that she found herself rereading.

*As my daughter sleeps peacefully in her pack 'n play, her golden curls resting on her chubby face, I can't help but smile. I know I did the right thing. Her perfect little face tells me so. She is my whole life, and her name fits her perfectly. Victoria. She will rise victoriously over the life that I escaped. She will not be influenced by it, and it will have no power over her. Victoria will be successful and strong, and, above all, she will know she is loved. When I think of how happy she is, growing up free and joyful in Sapphire Beach, I know I got us out of there just in time, and I don't regret doing what I had to do to escape.*

Connie stared out through the glass slider and into the darkness of the night sky. This didn't sound like someone about to abandon her daughter. What exactly happened to this woman, who, much like Connie, was just trying to follow her dream?

# Chapter 3

AFTER A NIGHT OF TOSSING, turning, and strange dreams, Connie's eyes opened on Friday morning before the alarm on her phone was set to wake her. It took her a minute to remember that today was move-in day.

After a quick shower and an English muffin with peanut butter, she threw on a comfortable sundress and brought Ginger for walk. She took the time to enjoy a mug of breakfast tea before loading her car with some necessary items and heading straight to the storage unit, where she had arranged to meet the movers at 8:00 AM. Grace was planning to be in the shop when she arrived with the movers.

Connie had packed her car with a doggie bed for Ginger, along with extra food and water bowls and some chew toys, so she could have a spot all set up and ready for Ginger the next day. She also packed a couple of mint plants for all the iced tea she would be drinking, especially during those scorching summer days that would soon be upon them.

Two men, who introduced themselves as Kyle and Alex, arrived right on time in a truck that had the words "Big and Burley Movers" printed across the sides. Despite the fact that they appeared small and scrawny, rather than big and burley, they made quick work of emptying the storage unit.

Connie followed the Big and Burley boys to the store and had to laugh when she saw Grace fluttering around the shop, wiping surfaces that were already clean and singing her heart out. She smiled at the thought of how pleased Aunt Concetta would be knowing Grace had become such an important part of her life. In moments like these, it was as if she were standing right next to her, enjoying the scene every bit as much as Connie was.

The overstuffed red sofa was the first item off the truck. Connie directed Kyle and Alex to place it on the left side of the store toward the front where, along with a coffee table, two armchairs, and an area rug, it would create a comfortable seating area.

The long table and newly upholstered chairs, courtesy of Grace's handiwork, went on the other side of the store, in a large nook off to the right of the checkout area. Connie could already envision herself seated at the solid oak table, creating an array of jewelry pieces or guiding her future students as they worked on their own creations. As soon as the store was up and running, Connie's first plan of action was to begin holding jewelry-making classes for people of all levels.

Next, Connie had the movers place the dentistry cabinet, where she would store beads that she wanted easily accessible, near the table, and pile the boxes in the center of the store, around the checkout area.

By 11:00, everything was unloaded and set in place. Connie had even set up Ginger's little home-away-from-home outside the storage room at the back of the shop, where she would be both out of the way and within Connie's line of vision from the checkout counter.

Connie still had to unpack the boxes, set up and price her product, and hang some pictures and mirrors, but she could see the light at the end of the tunnel. The move had gone smoothly, except for a few nicks and scratches on the wall that resulted from some missteps on the part of the movers. But she wasn't worried about it, since she still had time to add it to the punch list for Steve and Brittany.

After the movers left, Connie and Grace took a seat on the sofa, where they could both take in the entire store and see the sidewalks and street through the large picture windows that comprised much of the front wall of the shop.

"The store looks beautiful," Grace said with a broad smile. "Congratulations again, honey."

Connie was so excited she could barely sit still. "To celebrate, I'm going to pick us up an early lunch at that sandwich shop down the street. I've been wanting to check it out."

Just as Connie stood up to grab her purse, her landlord, Mickey Miranda, entered the shop. His silver-gray hair was combed back on the sides, and his bronze skin gave away how much time he spent on the beach. He wore navy swim trunks and a white tank top with a beach towel hanging around his neck.

"Hey, Mickey," Connie said, using all her strength not to break into the 1980s song "Mickey" by Toni Basil.

"Hi, Connie," he said, joining her and Grace in the seating area. "I was on the beach this morning and saw the moving truck. I wanted to stop by and see if you needed anything."

"Thanks, but I think we're in good shape. While you're here, though, I'd like to introduce you to Grace Jenkins. She will be working with me in the store."

"It looks fantastic," Mickey said after shaking Grace's hand. "You should easily be ready for your grand opening. It's two weeks away, right?"

"Yes, two weeks from tomorrow. I hope you'll tell your friends about it and stop by."

"I'll give that job to my wife," he said. "She has the gift of gab, if you know what I mean. We're both thrilled to have this space rented out again after everything that happened."

"We were just talking about the previous owner last night." Connie decided not to mention the items she found under the floorboards.

Mickey shook his head and bit his lower lip. "Yes, that was such a tragedy."

"I can't help but wonder why she just up and left," Connie said. "Hopefully she's out there safe somewhere."

Mickey let out a nervous chuckle. "Well, by breaking the terms of her lease, even if she came back, the shop would still be yours, so don't you worry about that."

"Um, that's not what I meant," Connie said, a little surprised at his callousness toward his previous tenant who could possibly be in danger. Or worse. "It just seems strange that she would just leave her child behind like that. What do you suppose happened?"

Mickey sat down on one of the armchairs and let out a deep breath. "It's true, she loved that little girl, but I guess drugs make people do strange things," he said with a shrug. "Victoria's father, Jordan Sugrue, came by a couple of weeks before she went missing. He was concerned for his daughter. He claimed that Natasha had a history of drug use, and he had reason to believe she might be using again. He asked me to keep an eye on her and call him if I saw anything suspicious."

"Did you? See anything suspicious, I mean?" Connie asked.

Mickey tugged at the beach towel around his neck. "I popped in regularly but didn't notice anything unusual. Except for one night, after the store closed, when I found a drug needle in the shrubs out back. She was a little late with the rent on a few occasions before her disappearance, but business always looked pretty steady to me. Who knows? Maybe she was using her profits for drugs."

"Maybe she couldn't take the pressure of running a business and being a single mom and turned back to drugs," Grace interjected. "Unfortunately, it happens."

Connie thought about the ledger and the to-do list she found. According to the ledger, business was good. And one of the items on her list was to confront her accountant. Maybe there was a connection. If Natasha had reason to believe that her accountant was skimming money off the top of her business, that might explain why she felt the need to keep her own records. It's possible that something went wrong when Natasha confronted the accountant.

31

"I guess anything is possible," Connie said. She didn't want to reveal to Mickey the information she had. "By the way, I'm looking for a good accountant to keep my books. Do you happen to know anyone?"

"A lot of people around here use Tracy Peterson," Mickey said. "I think she did Natasha's books. I have her number if you'd like."

"That would be great." There was no way Connie was going to hire Tracy, but this might provide her with the chance to get some information.

Before leaving, Mickey wrote down Tracy's phone number and address on a piece of paper Connie had fished out of her purse, and she thanked him for his help.

When Mickey left, Connie went out to get sandwiches for Grace and her and brought them back to the shop, where Grace was opening boxes and unwrapping pictures, mirrors, and other items that Connie had saved to potentially hang in the shop.

"Grace, you have done far more than your share of work. Please, just relax."

"Oh, sweetie, I'm happy to do it. I keep thinking how proud Concetta would be to see this shop."

Tears stung Connie's eyes. She put her arm around Grace's shoulders, and they sat down for lunch at the large table.

"Why all the questions for your landlord?" Grace asked, while they munched on their sandwiches. Connie got turkey and swiss with avocado and Grace tried the grilled chicken with Brie cheese and green apple. The sandwich shop was definitely a keeper.

Although Connie had told her friends at dinner last night about the items she had found under the loose floorboards, at that point Connie hadn't yet read the contents, so she caught Grace up to speed on the details. She read from her phone a few entries from Natasha's diary, where her love for her daughter was apparent.

"Mickey had a point," Grace said. "Drugs can make people do things they otherwise would never consider."

Connie swallowed the last bite of her sandwich. "True, but what if there's more to the story? Victoria will want answers when she gets older about what happened to her mother, and she deserves to have them."

"She most certainly does, but you gave everything to the police. I'm sure they will do everything they possibly can to find those answers."

*I'm sure they will,* Connie thought, *but a few casual conversations of my own couldn't hurt.*

# Chapter 4

AFTER LUNCH, THE WOMEN spent a few more hours unpacking boxes before collapsing into the nearest chair. The upholstered seats were far more comfortable than the metal ones from yesterday, and the table provided a solid surface to lean on.

"I can't look at another box," Connie said, lifting her head to meet Grace's tired gaze. "Let's call it a day."

Grace's weary expression, as she nodded in agreement, said it all.

However, their plans for a quick exit were interrupted when another visitor came through the door.

"I hope it's this busy when we open," Connie jokingly whispered to Grace.

"I come bearing gifts," their visitor said with a friendly smile. His head was shaved, and he wore a black tank top that revealed well-defined shoulders and biceps. This guy definitely hit the gym on a daily basis. An impressive tattoo of an eagle in flight on his left arm caught Connie's eye. She thought she remembered passing him on the street a few times but hadn't officially met him.

He handed Connie and Grace each a green smoothie. "I'm Gallagher McKeon," he said. "I own *Gallagher's Tropical Shack*, the restaurant and bar across the street. Or *The Shack*, as it is affectionately referred to."

Connie loved the exotic feel that the thatched roof on Gallagher's restaurant added to her view.

"Thanks," she said, introducing herself and Grace while she happily accepted the smoothie. "What's in them?"

"Almond milk, lots of leafy greens, and some apple with a touch of honey to cut the bitterness. I saw the moving truck leave this morning and noticed you've been working all day, so I thought you could use an afternoon pick-me-up."

"You look like a healthy young man," Grace said. "If it works for you, I'm willing to give it a try."

Connie placed her hand on Grace's shoulder. "Don't let Grace fool you. This young lady does mini-triathlons. She could out-exercise me anytime."

Gallagher put his right hand over his heart. "I'm impressed."

"This is pretty good," Connie said, holding up the half-emptied cup. "I think I feel the energy kicking in already. Do you sell them next door?"

"We do offer them, but we don't sell a lot. We attract more of an adult-beverage-type crowd. But I keep them on the menu to give people a healthy option. I like to keep fit, and they help me get those extra nutrients for my workouts."

"Well, I'll certainly be coming by for another," Connie said.

After chatting for a few minutes, Gallagher excused himself so he could help his staff prepare for the dinner rush, and Connie and Grace locked up shop. It was a little after 3:00 PM, and Connie was thrilled to have the rest of the day to herself. It would be a much-needed reprieve in the middle of a busy several months, and the warm sun and saltwater were beckoning.

The year-round sunshine of southwest Florida was one of the factors that had always attracted Connie to the area. While her aunt was still alive, she would often try to get away in February or March, even if only for a long weekend, for that cherished dose of vitamin D.

After completing her one-mile commute down Sapphire Beach Boulevard, Connie parked in her designated spot in the underground garage. She climbed the stairs to the luxurious lobby of Palm Paradise and made her way across the marble floor to check her mailbox. Just bills and junk mail. Then she stopped to say a quick hello to Jessica, the condo management representative who kept on-site office hours, and went up to her condo, where she received a hero's welcome from Ginger. After taking her for a long walk, Connie changed into her bathing suit.

She felt slightly guilty about leaving Ginger again, but she couldn't leave the dog unattended on the beach while she swam. "Don't worry, sweet girl, I won't be long, and tomorrow you get to come to the shop with me."

It was Connie's favorite time of day for a swim. Although the sun was no longer at its peak, it still shone strongly in the sky. She followed the cement pathway that brought her from the main entrance to the lobby around to the back of the building, past the pool area, and onto the silky white sands of Sapphire Beach.

Connie spread her towel across the soft sand and sat with her face turned toward the warmth of the sun. As she watched a paddle boarder glide along the coast, Connie promised herself she would purchase her own board as soon as possible. Ever since Elyse introduced her to the sport in January, she was hooked. But for now, a swim would do just fine.

She chuckled to herself thinking of Elyse's not-so-subtle attempts to convince her to relocate to Sapphire Beach instead of going with her original plan to sell her aunt's condo. *I guess Elyse got the last laugh on that one.*

Connie waded into the water until she was hip deep, then leaned back, as though falling into a giant green pillow. She side-stroked her way to the swimmers' lane, where she could swim some laps without bothering those splashing around near the shore.

When she got a little further out, Connie switched to the crawl stroke. Focusing only on the sound of her breathing and the cool water against her body, she tuned out everything else. Within a few minutes, her head began to clear, and her body relaxed. The reaching motion of the crawl stroke stretched the muscles in her arms and torso, stiff from all the cleaning and unpacking. After about twenty minutes of swimming, she rolled onto her back and allowed the waves to carry her back to shore.

She wasn't quite ready to get out, so she sat in the shallow water and let the gentle waves crash over her body. It didn't take long for her thoughts, like wood floating on a gentle wave, to drift towards Natasha.

Connie couldn't help but feel a connection to the young mother. Perhaps it was because they each pursued a dream that led them to the same shop in Sapphire Beach - Natasha as a boutique owner who wanted a better life for her baby daughter, and Connie as a jewelry maker who believed she could help provide a better life for families in developing countries by selling their creations.

Or maybe Connie was just letting sentimentality get the best of her. After all, Victoria's father said that Natasha struggled with addiction, and he had concerns that she was using again. And Mickey had found a drug needle in the bushes behind the shop.

But that was only circumstantial evidence. It could have belonged to anyone who decided to hide behind the shops after hours to do drugs.

Judging from Natasha's diary, Connie saw no indications of anything beyond a mother who would do whatever it took to give her child a good life. She even apparently fled from something in her past to protect her daughter. Connie wondered if Victoria's father was part of what she had run from. If he was, and it had been as bad as her diary indicated, then nothing he said could be trusted.

Then there was Natasha's accountant, Tracy, with whom she had had some type of confrontation shortly before her disappearance. Was that connected to the accounting ledger Natasha kept? According to Natasha's records, she was turning a pretty good profit. So, if not because of drugs, then why was she late with her rent, as Mickey had said? Maybe

41

Natasha confronted Tracy, and the encounter went bad.

Or it could be something else altogether. Connie just had too little to go on. But one thing she did know: there were too many unanswered questions to assume she ran away.

At least she had Tracy's contact information. Maybe she could learn something by talking to her. And Gallagher seemed friendly. Being right across the street, perhaps he had some insight.

Satisfied that she had had enough of the water for one day, and not wanting to leave Ginger alone much longer, Connie toweled off and went back upstairs. She heated up some leftovers and relaxed on the couch for the rest of the evening.

\*\*\*

On Saturday morning, Connie woke up refreshed from her afternoon off and headed straight into the shop with Ginger in tow. Since she would mostly be unpacking boxes of displays and jewelry, Connie had insisted that Grace take the day off. She had already been more than generous with her time.

Ginger loved her doggie area, which contained her bed, a few toys, and bowls for water and food. Connie had strategically placed it near the storage room, so that if Ginger wished to escape from the activity of the shop, she could hide out there, or if she preferred, she would be free to roam about.

Pulling up her favorite playlist on her phone for ambiance, Connie got to work opening boxes and spreading their contents on various product shelves throughout the store. She had photos of her artisans and landscapes of the countries where they lived. The artisans were a huge part of the shop, and since they couldn't be there in person, she wanted to make sure their photos had a prominent spot. Which reminded her, she needed to be sure Steve or Brittany hung them up when they returned to the shop. She pulled out her phone and shot Steve a quick text.

Then she unpacked some small handwoven baskets and carved wooden statues of animals she had chosen from her Kenyan collection and arranged them haphazardly between the jewelry displays in the Fair Trade section. Once the shelves were stocked with jewelry, she'd take more time to accessorize them, but for now she just wanted to empty the boxes.

By late morning, Connie was ready for a break. Reaching into her pocket, she fished out the piece of paper with Tracy's phone number and address. Now was as good a time as any.

# Chapter 5

TRACY WORKED FROM AN OFFICE in her home, so even though it was Saturday, Connie hoped she might still be there. After attaching Ginger's leash and locking up the store, Connie and her little sidekick made the short walk to the car. The GPS took them to one of the side streets off the main boulevard, not too far from where Stephanie lived. Tracy's neighborhood was filled with comfy-looking bungalows that were only a short walk to the beach.

When Connie arrived at the house, she pulled her car in front of Tracy's mermaid mailbox and took Ginger with her up to the house. The dog would give her a good excuse not to stay long if anything didn't feel right.

Connie hesitated at the sound of a familiar masculine voice coming through the door. Where had she heard that voice before? She pressed her finger into the black wrought iron doorbell and was greeted by a woman who looked to be in her late thirties with a medium build and dark curls that fell just above her shoulders.

Mickey Miranda was peeking out from behind her.

He quickly explained to Tracy that Connie was a new business owner in town and that he had recommended her as an accountant.

In reality, Connie's father was an accountant and had offered to take care of her accounting needs free of charge, calling it a win-win. "I can both support my daughter's venture," he had said, "and also contribute to a great cause." But Mickey and Tracy didn't need to know that.

"Actually, I'm planning to wait until the business is off the ground before hiring anyone," Connie explained to Tracy, "but I just thought I'd put out some feelers sooner rather than later."

"I was just on my way out," Mickey said. Then, holding Tracy's gaze, he said, "You be sure to treat her fairly."

Mickey's comment struck Connie as odd. Was it just an expression, or was Tracy in the habit of treating people unfairly?

Tracy invited Connie inside while she got a list of her services and rates.

Connie waited in the foyer, admiring some photos on the wall, while Tracy disappeared down the hallway. Within a couple of minutes, she had returned with a professional-looking list in hand.

"This must be your sister," Connie said, pointing to one of the photos that hung above a half moon table in the foyer. "The two of you look so much alike."

Tracy swallowed hard. "Yes, that's Tiffany. But we haven't seen each other in a while." For a moment her thoughts seemed a million miles away, but she quickly regained her composure as she handed Connie the list.

"Do you mind if we talk outside?" Connie asked, motioning toward two blue Adirondack chairs in the front yard. "I wouldn't want Ginger here to track dirt into your living room." She felt safer knowing that at least Mickey knew where she was. That is, unless Mickey was on Team Tracy.

"Of course," she said, leading the way to the chairs.

As soon as Connie sat, Ginger jumped on her lap.

"These rates seem fair." Actually, from what she knew of her father's business, they seemed pretty low. Hopefully that wasn't because Tracy made up the difference by pilfering money from clients.

"Thank you for this," Connie said, folding it and putting it in her pocket. "I will be in touch as soon as I am ready to talk business. As I said earlier, for now I'm just focusing on getting up and running. I'm still learning my way around. In fact," Connie said, looking directly at Tracy, "I just heard what happened to poor Natasha Orlov. I understand she was a client of yours."

Tracy's eyes widened for a moment. "Yes," she said after a brief pause, "such a tragedy. Business had been a little slow. I guess the pressure got to her."

"It seems strange that she would just take off, given she was so committed to her business and her daughter," Connie said. "Do you know of anyone who might have wanted to harm her?"

Tracy gaze was so intense that it felt like she was looking straight through Connie. It gave her the feeling she was being sized up. "I think it's more likely that she ran away. But then again," she added, "it could have been her landlord."

Connie's shocked expression must have spoken for itself. It didn't take long for Tracy to throw Mickey under the bus.

"Between you and me, Natasha was falling further and further behind on her rent, and he had warned her that if she didn't catch up soon, he would take action. She kept talking her way into more time, but he was losing patience."

Mickey had said that Natasha was late a couple of times, but according to him, she had been caught up by the time she disappeared. Of course, if Mickey had been involved in Natasha's disappearance, he might not want to reveal his motive.

Since Connie had already come this far, she decided to bite the bullet and ask her burning question. "Tracy, I found some information that seemed to indicate that Natasha's store was doing pretty well financially. There was also a note that she was going to confront you about stealing money from her. I only ask, because, if we are going to do business together, I want to make sure I can trust those on my team." The note never mentioned stealing money, but Connie wanted to gauge Tracy's reaction.

Ginger stirred in her lap, but she reassured the dog by stroking her soft coat. She had her car keys in the other hand, just in case she wanted to leave quickly.

"Look," Tracy said, "it's hard running a business for the first time, and, while Natasha had experience in retail, she had to overcome a steep learning curve for other aspects of the job. She simply wasn't earning enough to turn a decent profit. Some months she had to choose between paying Mickey the rent and taking a salary. As a young mother, I'm sure she did what she needed to do."

"So, you think that she ran away to escape financial problems?"

"It's not out of the realm of possibility. Or maybe Mickey decided to take matters into his own hands and expedite the process."

Connie was finding herself hoping that Natasha had indeed run away, because, if Tracy was telling the truth, the alternative was that her landlord was a killer.

She couldn't think of any more questions, so she thanked Tracy for her time and left. On the way back to the shop, Connie stopped for a quick sandwich, then spent the rest of the afternoon unpacking the last of the boxes that the movers had delivered. Then she moved on to the ones in the storeroom, which contained Fair Trade jewelry from Kenya and Ecuador, and carefully placed it on the displays. Inside each piece of tissue paper was another unique treasure, making her feel like a child on Christmas morning. She hoped the Sapphire Beach clientele would love them as much as she did.

As Connie worked, Ginger settled into a comfy spot on the plush, white area rug under the glass coffee table by the couch and only stirred to follow Connie out back when she went to grab more boxes of jewelry.

After unpacking the last box, Connie sat on the couch with a bottle of water. Ginger lazily lifted her head, then went back to sleep, apparently deciding it wasn't worth the effort to hop onto the couch.

"So, you shed your white-and-chestnut-colored fur all over my shop, then ignore me?" she teased the dog.

Connie had to laugh at Ginger's token tail-wag.

The sound of the door chime pulled Connie's attention away from her four-legged friend. It was Zach, and he looked more tired than she felt.

"Hi, Zach. It's good to see you." She couldn't help but wonder if his unexpected visit was a social call or connected to police business. She found herself hoping it was the former. She started to get up, but he motioned for her not to bother and took a seat in the armchair facing her.

"It looks fantastic in here," he said, craning his neck to look around the store. His eyes settled on a painting of Sapphire Beach with a parasailer floating across the blue sky, which was temporarily leaning against a wall. Zach had given it to Connie as a memento the night before she went home to Boston, before he knew she had made the decision to relocate to Sapphire Beach.

She followed his gaze over to the picture. "I was thinking of hanging it over there," she said, pointing to the driftwood accent wall. "I think the colors will really pop against the gray wood."

"It'll look fantastic there," he said with a wide grin. "That's kind of why I stopped by," he continued.

"To visit your painting?" she said, grinning.

"Very funny. No, I was wondering if I could take you parasailing if you'd still like to go. I remember you saying it was on your bucket list when we talked in January, so I was hoping you might like to go with me."

Connie was surprised he remembered that from their conversation. It had only been three months, but it felt like ages ago.

"I know it's a busy time for you, but I don't imagine it will be less busy once the store opens," he added.

He was right. Life would always be busy, and she had promised herself she would take the time to slow down and enjoy life. And it seemed like that should include getting to know Zach. "That sounds like fun. I'd love to."

"Great. Are you free next Sunday? I have the day off."

"Next Sunday is perfect."

"Would early afternoon work?" Zach asked. "I usually go to a later Mass, so I can sleep in."

Connie was pleasantly surprised that he attended Mass. She hadn't seen him there in January, but she had gone to an earlier Mass the Sunday she was in town.

"Sounds good. I will probably see you there."

"Great," he said. "I'll look for you."

He stood up to leave, and Connie walked him to the door.

"By the way," Connie asked, "did the information I found bring about any leads in Natasha's disappearance?"

He shook his head. "I usually don't work Saturdays, but I spent today looking into a few things. So far nothing solid. Besides Natasha's ledger, there isn't anything that points to Tracy embezzling money."

"That's too bad," Connie said. "I was really hoping for some answers, for her daughter's sake."

"Me, too. It's definitely a sad one," he said.

# Chapter 6

ZACH LEFT AS BRITTANY was coming in. He stopped to hold the door for her and nodded as she went past him.

"See you soon," Zach said, waving at Connie on his way out. Then he entered the police vehicle parked in front of Connie's store.

"I hope everything is okay," Brittany said, gesturing toward the police car as Zach pulled away. "Why were the police here?"

"There's nothing to worry about. Zach just stopped by to see how the store was coming along," she said, not wanting to overshare.

"Steve called and asked if I could come by to finish a few projects. Is now a good time to work on that punch list?"

"Your timing is perfect. I also have some pictures I'd love you to hang. Oh, and the movers left a few scratches on the wall over there that need to be repaired," Connie said, pointing to a wall near the table.

"No problem. I'll have this all done in no time," Brittany said.

Connie sat at the table and observed as Brittany touched up the wall. Then she showed her where the pictures should be hung.

"I don't mean to watch over your shoulder," Connie said, "but I'm so jealous. I have no knack for this kind of stuff at all."

"It's easier than it looks. Here, let me show you," Brittany said. She offered Connie some tips on measuring and hanging pictures as she worked.

"You make it look easy. I guarantee I'd have a few extra holes in the wall."

The young woman laughed. "Nah, it just takes patience and believing in yourself. We have the power within us to do what we think is impossible if we set our mind to it."

Connie wondered if Brittany had ever been a motivational speaker or life coach. She always seemed to interject some wisdom into the conversation.

"Maybe, but I think a little talent helps, too. If you saw some of my projects, I think you might agree," she said with a wink.

"Fair enough," Brittany said, grinning as she hammered. "But I promise, with a little practice you'd be surprised at what you can do."

"I think I'll just call you for my carpentry needs. It will save us both a lot of grief, since you won't have to fix all *my* fixes."

"Actually, you'll have to call Steve. I'm moving back home to be with my boyfriend next month."

"That's too bad. I enjoy having a woman carpenter," Connie said. "But I wish you the best of luck."

Brittany had hung all the photos and was about halfway through the rest of the punch list when her phone pinged.

"It's Steve. He needs me on another project, but I promise to be back to finish up before the grand opening."

After Brittany left, Connie decided that she and Ginger needed to get outside to stretch their legs and enjoy the beautiful day. The temperature had been averaging in the high eighties, and there wasn't a cloud in the bright blue Florida sky.

They strolled toward the beach, still packed with tourists and residents, and Connie spotted Gallagher having an early dinner on a bench.

"Who do we have here?" he said, giving Ginger a scratch behind the ears while she basked in the attention.

"This is my new BFF named Ginger," she said. "She belonged to my aunt who recently passed away."

Connie glanced down at Gallagher's meal, which consisted of a large salad with grilled chicken, plenty of greens and sprouts, and a purplish smoothie. "Looks healthy. I wish I had the discipline to eat that well." While Connie more or less chose healthy foods, she had more than her fair share of splurges. "Have you always been this healthy?"

Gallagher shook his head and laughed. "This is relatively new. I used to be everything *but* healthy. Too much alcohol and other things that I don't like to think about."

"I love ice cream and burgers way too much. I can't imagine giving them up."

"Everybody's got to find their own balance," he said. "I tend to go to extremes in whatever I do, so this is my way of going to a healthy extreme."

Connie glanced down the street to *Gallagher's Tropical Shack*. "You don't find it difficult to own a restaurant and bar and not eat the food or drink?" she asked.

"I'm just grateful to be living my dream. The restaurant has been something I've wanted as long as I can remember, and I have no intention of doing anything to mess it up." There was a sadness in his eyes as he spoke, which she didn't remember seeing when she first met him.

With Gallagher's encouragement, Connie sat down and shared a little about herself, as well, and the circumstances that led her to open *Just Jewelry*, while he finished his salad and smoothie. She found him positive and easy to talk to, and she was happy that he was her neighbor.

Since Gallagher was so friendly, he probably befriended Natasha, as well. She decided to broach the subject delicately, in case they had been friends.

"I was so sorry to hear what happened to Natasha Orlov," she said. "Did you know her well?"

His expression transformed from relaxed to serious, and he quickly shook his head. "No, we were just neighbors."

Still, his restaurant was directly across the street. "It seems strange that a young mother with ties to the area would vanish into thin air. Did you ever see anything suspicious going on in her shop?"

Gallagher swallowed hard and looked up towards the green and blue waters of the Gulf of Mexico. "I couldn't say, but I would leave it alone if I were you." Then he turned and looked intently at Connie. "I wouldn't want to see you getting hurt. Or worse."

It felt more like concern than a threat, but Connie was taken aback by his strong words and sudden change in demeanor.

"Maybe you're right," she said.

Gallagher's shoulders relaxed as he gave Ginger a small piece of chicken and then got up to throw away his empty food container. "I'd better be getting back. It's almost Saturday evening, so the restaurant should be filling up, knock on wood," he said, gently tapping on his own head with his knuckles. He seemed to be back to his congenial self.

Gallagher sipped on the remainder of his smoothie while they walked together back in the direction of their businesses.

When she got back to the shop, Connie decided to call it a day. She had plans to meet Elyse and Stephanie for dinner later at *Surfside Restaurant* on the beach, and she wanted to get a quick workout in at the building's exercise room.   for a while went a long way in keeping up with her martial arts skills and releasing a little stress.

After a cool shower, Connie slipped into a smoky-blue sleeveless dress, perfect for a late March evening in Sapphire Beach, and chose a silver and beige leather-wrapped necklace and matching bracelet, which she had made last year, to accessorize her dress. Then she headed back downtown to *Surfside Restaurant*, where Elyse and Stephanie were already seated at a prime outdoor table overlooking the beach. As she stepped onto the deck, it was as if she was looking at a canvas with pale blue waters painted against a bright orange sky.

It was the perfect backdrop for a relaxing evening with friends.

At the table next to them was a couple with a baby cooing in its carrier. The women couldn't help but stare at the adorable little guy laughing as his father made funny faces at him. They complimented the proud parents and went back to studying their menus.

Connie noticed a far-away expression on Elyse's face.

"Are you remembering when Emma was that little?" she said, calling Elyse back to the present moment.

She shook her head and wiped a tear from her eyes. "Kind of," Elyse said, shifting in her chair. "It's just, I've always wanted to have siblings for Emma, but after she was born, the doctors informed us we couldn't have any more children. Josh and I were devastated but also grateful to have Emma. We had met in high school and married right out of college, so I'd always imagined that we would have a large family."

Connie squeezed Elyse's hand, and Stephanie got up to give her a hug.

"I'm so sorry to hear that," Stephanie said. "I never knew."

"Most of the time, I'm okay. It's just, once in a while..." she trailed off, her eyes settling again on the baby.

Elyse's revelation set the tone for the evening, and the women spent the rest of the night talking about their own hopes and dreams, some fulfilled, others not.

Stephanie shared that she, too, had wanted children, but she married in her thirties and soon became aware that her marriage was not going to last. "The infidelity started early, and I wasn't going to bring a child into that situation. I was already too angry, and our home wouldn't have been a healthy environment to raise a child."

After some words of compassion from Connie and Elyse, she added, "But I do find a lot of fulfillment in my work as a physical therapist. I mostly work with the elderly here in Florida, but at times I also have the chance to help children. I may not have worked full-time if I had a family and, I don't know, it may sound corny, but everything just feels right when I am helping someone regain their mobility and their life along with it."

As the night wore on, Connie told them that she had a date with Zach the following weekend.

"What a shocker," Stephanie said, sarcastically.

Elyse was thrilled at the idea of Connie dating one of her husband's good friends, and they both made Connie promise to keep them posted.

Eventually, the conversation turned to Natasha's disappearance. Connie told the women that she had talked to Mickey, Gallagher, and Tracy since they last spoke a few days ago, just after she had found the box of evidence. "I just can't stop myself from digging around for more information," she said. "Being in the same shop where Natasha worked makes it hard to avoid thinking about it."

"That's not exactly surprising to me," Elyse said. "I had a feeling you wouldn't be able to let it go. Then when you found the box under the floorboards, I knew there was no chance of you staying out of it completely."

"So, what are your thoughts on the case?" Stephanie asked.

After recapping the gist of her conversation with Tracy, Connie said, "I haven't ruled out the possibility that Natasha confronted Tracy about skimming money from the business and threatened to go to the police. If that happened, Tracy could have killed her and hid the body. But then, just before I left, Tracy tried to throw suspicion on Mickey, claiming that Natasha was behind on rent, and he wanted her out of his building, maybe enough to kill her."

"Mickey Miranda, your landlord?" Elyse asked. "I hope it's not him. I'll never forgive myself if I put you in a dangerous situation."

Connie pretended to be surprised. "You mean you forgot to ask Mickey if he's in the habit of killing his tenants if they are late with the rent?"

Elyse gave her a sarcastic smile. "I was going to ask, but he offered such a good deal that I figured it would be worth the risk."

"That's why you're my realtor."

"Do you really think it could be Mickey?" Stephanie asked. "That would have been a bit extreme on Mickey's part."

"Natasha's to-do list did say to call Mickey. But I suppose that could be about anything. It's not unusual to call your landlord."

"What did he say when you talked to him?" Elyse asked.

"Mickey thinks it was drugs. He said that Victoria's father, Jordan Sugrue, claimed that Natasha had a drug problem, and he suspected she was using again. Mickey said he found a drug needle outside the store. But then, in her diary, Natasha talked about running away from something in her past, so if Jordan was part of what she was trying to escape, he could have been lying to Mickey."

"Or Mickey could have been lying about finding the drug needle," Stephanie said.

"Jordan Sugrue," Elyse said. "That name sounds familiar."

"Maybe Josh mentioned him in connection with the case," Connie suggested.

"I don't think so. He doesn't usually talk about the details of his cases, and besides, this case has been on the backburner since their leads ran dry last summer," Elyse said. "Even with the new evidence you found, they still don't have anything solid."

Connie was disappointed to hear that they were no longer actively investigating.

"You said you talked to your neighbor," Stephanie asked. "Did he say anything interesting?"

"When I ran into Gallagher McKeon this afternoon and asked him if he ever saw anything suspicious at Natasha's store, he got all weird on me. He is usually super friendly, so I got the feeling he was hiding something."

"Maybe he was friends with Natasha, and it's hard for him to talk about it," Stephanie said.

"Except that he specifically said that they *weren't* friends."

Elyse let out a deep breath. "Whatever you do next, just be careful. You don't know who you can trust."

# Chapter 7

MUCH TO CONNIE'S ANNOYANCE, at 7:00 on Sunday morning, she was wide awake. After rolling over and trying to will herself back to sleep for a little while, she decided to go with it and attend an earlier Mass. She had determined to stay away from *Just Jewelry* for the day, since it would be harder to get a Sunday off once the store opened, and she was ahead of schedule in preparing for the grand opening.

Inspired by Gallagher's creations, she pulled together some fruit, blended it with vanilla almond milk, and made a smoothie for breakfast. It wasn't quite as good as his, but it did the trick. After taking Ginger for a leisurely walk along Sapphire Beach Boulevard, she got ready and headed to Our Lady, Star of the Sea parish for the 9:00 Mass.

After taking a seat towards the front of the church, her thoughts drifted to Victoria. She was saying a prayer that the little girl was well cared for, when Elyse slid into the pew and took the seat next to Connie, followed by Emma, Josh, and Gertrude. As Elyse asked in a whispered tone what Connie was doing for the rest of the day, Connie smiled and waved at the others, then told Elyse she was thinking about renting a paddleboard for a couple of hours later that afternoon. "I'm planning to buy one when I have time to research a good board, but for today, I just wanted to get out onto the water."

"I have an open house after Mass, but I'd be happy to take you this afternoon to where Josh and I bought ours," Elyse said. "You remember Ashley and Travis? They have a little shop where they sell paddleboards and kayaks, and they usually have some great used boards for sale. You can always get a fancier one later, when you have more experience."

Connie smiled at the mention of Ashley and Travis. They were a young couple from the Boston area who bought Sapphire Beach Boat Rentals and relocated to southwest Florida. When Elyse had taken Connie paddleboarding in January, Elyse had used them to discretely drop the hint to Connie that she should consider keeping Concetta's condo and moving to Sapphire Beach.

At the time, Connie hadn't yet thought of the idea of selling Fair Trade jewelry, so she was still planning to sell the condo. Although it had only been a few months, it seemed like a lifetime ago that she and Elyse first stood in the shop that would become *Just Jewelry*.

"I would love that, but are you sure? I don't want to cut into your family time."

"Emma and Josh have plans to play beach volleyball together - it's Emma's new passion - so I have the time. Besides," she said, "it's the least I can do, since I'm the one who got you hooked in the first place. I'll meet you at your place around 1:00."

"Perfect," Connie said, standing for the processional hymn.

When Mass ended, Connie waited a few minutes until the crowds cleared out, hoping to be able to speak with the pastor, Fr. Paul Fulton, for a few minutes. It was the first time she had seen him since deciding to move to Sapphire Beach, and he was ecstatic to learn of her decision.

He peppered her with questions, eager to learn how she came to the decision and went about finding Fair Trade artisans, and she was eager to tell him the story, because it was one of his homilies in January that nudged her along in her decision.

Having spent many years in the missions, Fr. Paul loved the idea of selling Fair Trade items and promised to come to the grand opening to buy a gift for his sister. He also ensured her of his ongoing prayers for her family after losing Concetta.

After stopping for groceries, Connie settled into the spare bedroom, where she had a folding table and some comfy chairs set up for jewelry making and went to work on a layered necklace she hoped to have completed in time for the grand opening.

Connie was so excited about the paddleboard that, by the time Elyse called up from the lobby, she had put away her work and was pacing the living room just waiting for her to arrive.

"I'm too excited to even invite you up," she said, through the intercom. "Do you mind if we head right out?"

Elyse laughed. "Just buzz me in, and I'll wait for you in the lobby."

Their first stop was a sporting goods store to purchase a mounting device for Connie's Jetta, so she could transport her new paddleboard home, as well as to other beaches if she wanted to venture away from her back yard. Fortunately, there were plenty of inexpensive options, especially since she only planned to go a short distance. She also purchased a dolly for transporting it from her storage bin in the underground garage to the beach.

The next stop was Travis's and Ashley's shop. Normally, they would both be on the beach tending to their rental business, but Ashley had just stopped in to check on their employee, and she was ecstatic to learn of Connie's relocation. Connie gave her the brief version of the story and promised to stop by another time to visit.

With Elyse's and Ashley's help, Connie was able to get a deal on a gently used board and paddle that was perfect for a beginner. A smile spread across Connie's face as she pulled out her debit card to purchase the powder-blue paddleboard, paddle, and matching life vest. Although a part of her hated to spend even a little money on luxury items before her business got off the ground, she could almost hear her Aunt Concetta's voice echoing in her mind: "Life is not a dress rehearsal."

After all, what good was living in paradise if she couldn't take full advantage of all that it had to offer? She couldn't wait to get out on the water and promised herself that, at least once a week, she would set her alarm a little earlier for a paddle down the beach.

When they got back to Palm Paradise, Elyse insisted on accompanying her to the water to see her off on what Elyse had dubbed her maiden voyage. They went upstairs just long enough for Connie to change into her bathing suit and beach coverup and grab a towel. Then they unloaded the board from the top of Connie's car, fastened it into the dolly, and Connie proudly pulled it to the beach.

Leaving her coverup, towel, and the dolly on the sand, Connie fastened her life vest and paddled away from shore. After a few seconds, she unsteadily turned around to wave at Elyse, who waved back, laughing as she left. It was only her second time on a paddleboard, so it was touch and go for a little while, especially when jet skis passing in the distance sent a flurry of waves in her direction. Turning around proved to be the hardest, and she ended up in the water a few times, but overall, Connie was pretty pleased with herself. The saltwater on her skin and the fresh air in her lungs felt amazing. Relocating had undoubtedly been the right decision.

As happy as she was to be out on the water, after about an hour, her burning shoulder muscles told her it was time to head in. She still had a lot of physical work to do in the store the following day, and she didn't want to be too sore.

After putting her new toy and its accessories in the storage closet behind her parking space, she went back upstairs, where she received an enthusiastic greeting from Ginger. She fixed herself a homemade pizza with some fresh dough and veggies she had bought earlier and put it in the oven to cook while she fed Ginger and showered off the sand and salt. Then she took Ginger for a walk while the pizza cooled.

When she returned, she poured herself a generous glass of Merlot, took her pizza onto the balcony, and ate while overlooking the Gulf of Mexico.

Connie had never dreamed she would be living this type of lifestyle at thirty-four: a condo on the beach, her own shop, and not stressing over money. Working for a non-profit her whole life, she had always lived frugally. It was still a new experience to be able to afford luxuries, such as her stand-up paddleboard.

After dinner, Connie texted Elyse a selfie she had taken with her new board in the background with the message, *Thanks for all your help today. You're the best!*

A few minutes later, Elyse responded, *My pleasure,* with a smiley face emoji.

With the evening in front of her and nothing on the agenda, Connie decided to reread Natasha's diary to study it more closely. Maybe a second read-through would provide some fresh insight. She pulled the printouts from the drawer of one of her end tables and settled onto the couch with Ginger on her lap.

Reading Natasha's diary was like looking through a window into her life, but one with an obstructed view. Some things about her were evident, while she seemed to talk about others in a veiled manner. She felt as if Natasha were reaching out to her from wherever she was, but in code rather than in plain English.

However, one thing was consistently clear - the love she had for Victoria. Once again, it didn't seem possible that Natasha would have abandoned her daughter. Of course, if she did struggle with addiction, that could be a powerful force that caused people to do things outside their normal character. So, it was impossible to be certain.

As Connie continued to study the diary, she noticed that several times Natasha referred to a close friend and confidant called Mac.

*I remember when I told Mac that I named my daughter Victoria to symbolize that my child would be victorious over the past,* Natasha had written. *He was so inspired by my reason for choosing that name that, once our nightmare was finally over, he got a tattoo of a majestic eagle. He said it would remind him of how we soared above so many challenges.*

As she came to the end of the last entry, a yawn stretched open her mouth, and she decided to call it a night. *It must be the paddleboarding,* she thought. *I guess I'm not as fit as I thought.*

She returned the journal to the drawer and dropped into bed with the image of an eagle swirling around in her mind.

# Chapter 8

THE NEXT FEW DAYS FLEW BY, as Connie, with Grace's faithful assistance, devoted her time to arranging product displays and merchandise throughout the shop. She gave the Fair Trade section a prime spot between the larger of the two front display windows and the red sofa. With a little over a week until the grand opening, there was still a lot of work left to do, but Connie was confident that it would get done in plenty of time.

Despite her insistence that Grace take the day off, on Thursday morning they were back in the shop working side by side.

Towards the end of the morning, Grace took a walk to get some fresh air, while Connie snapped pictures of the store's progress, along with some close-ups of an array of jewelry to post on social media. She was perusing the photos on her phone when a young woman with blond hair that reached halfway down the length of her back stepped inside and looked around the store.

Grace returned from her walk as the woman entered the shop.

"Hi," Connie said, with a friendly smile. "We haven't opened yet, but I'd be happy to tell you about *Just Jewelry*."

"I know you don't open until next Saturday, but I've seen the contractors and moving van, and I've been dying to see what you're doing in here. My name is Penelope," she said, extending her hand. "I work for Gallagher now, but I used to work for Natasha back when this was *Natasha's Boutique*."

"In that case, welcome back," Connie said, introducing herself and Grace. "I'm so sorry for your loss."

Tears filled Penelope's eyes, and she looked away.

Connie led the young woman over to the sofa, then took a seat in the armchair facing her, while Grace brought over three bottles of water and pulled a package of tissue from her purse.

"Thank you," she said, accepting a water from Grace and taking a tissue from the package. "I'm sorry. It's just that the last time I was in here, I was with Natasha." She dabbed her eyes.

"So, you knew her well?" Grace asked.

"She was my best friend. I miss her and Victoria so much."

Grace sat next to Penelope and squeezed her arm. "I'm so sorry, honey."

"Victoria's father won't even let me visit, not that I'd want to go to that place. But Jordan thought it was better for her to make a clean break from her life in Sapphire Beach."

"Where are Victoria and Jordan now?" Connie asked.

Penelope's thoughts seemed far away. "They're living in the Panhandle."

"I don't understand," Grace interjected. "Why wouldn't you want to go there?"

Fear flashed in Penelope's eyes, and her hands began to tremble. "He's just a horrible person. Natasha didn't want Victoria raised by him, but Jordan's her father, so he automatically got custody. There was nothing I could do."

Connie and Grace exchanged a confused glance.

Penelope wasn't making a lot of sense, but Connie didn't want to press it. The young woman seemed to be on the verge of breaking down.

"When was the last time you saw Victoria?" Connie asked.

"I haven't seen her since the night Natasha disappeared. Natasha had seemed preoccupied that week, and I wasn't surprised when she called me to see if I could watch the baby for a little while, so she could get away and think. It was a slow June day, and another employee was working at the store, so we both had the evening off. I always loved spending time with Victoria, so I was happy to do it. When Natasha hadn't returned by Victoria's bedtime, I started to get nervous. I put the baby down in my bed, and a few hours later, when she still didn't come back, I called the police."

"Do you have any idea what had been on her mind?" Connie asked.

Grace shot her a look, indicating she was being rude with so many questions, but Penelope didn't seem to mind. It looked like it was doing her good to talk about it, so Connie tried to pretend she didn't see Grace's hint.

"I know that she came to Sapphire Beach for a fresh start away from the baby's father. She definitely didn't want him in her life." Penelope, whose gaze had settled on a palm tree across the street, suddenly looked back at Connie. "Why are you so interested?"

Connie thought about mentioning the diary but didn't want to upset Penelope unnecessarily. She leaned back on the couch and searched her mind for another reason. "I guess it's because I, too, came to Sapphire Beach to fulfill a dream, and I kind of feel we were kindred spirits in that sense. I admire that she wanted a new life, different from whatever past she was looking to escape, and she seemed like a good mother. Since we share the same shop, I guess we have a built-in connection."

Penelope smiled. "Natasha was a great mom and a special person. She was a free spirit, although I get the sense she settled down when her daughter was born. I don't know a lot of the details about her life before Sapphire Beach, but I don't believe that she skipped town without Victoria. Some have mentioned a drug history, but I never saw any signs of that, and between working together and being friends, I was with her almost every day."

Connie smiled warmly. "Hopefully the police can solve the mystery. And if I figure anything out, I will let you know."

Penelope thanked her. "By the way, I love what you're doing here. I think handmade jewelry will do well in this town, and I love the Fair Trade angle. I will be sure to stop by the grand opening and tell my friends about it."

After she and Grace walked Penelope to the door, Connie took a seat at the large wooden table to work on advertising and her online presence but was distracted by Grace, who had followed her to the table and stood with her hands on her hips, glaring down at Connie.

"Can I help you?" Connie said, trying to suppress her laughter.

"Why all the questions about Natasha's disappearance? I want you to promise me you'll stay out of it and let the police handle it. Remember how you almost got killed in January when you investigated those murders at Palm Paradise?"

"There's nothing to worry about. I was just asking a few questions, and besides, it seemed to do Penelope some good to talk about it."

"Okay," Grace said, giving Connie a kiss on the top of her head. "I'm just watching out for you."

"I know," Connie said, "and I love you for it."

Since Connie planned to do computer work for the rest of the afternoon, she convinced Grace to take the rest of the day off. She spent the next couple of hours at the table uploading photos onto her social media accounts and the website.

One of the advantages to having worked at a small non-profit was that Connie had a lot of practice with various facets of running a business, so she knew how to design a website and maximize her exposure on social media. Now that she was starting her own business, she was grateful for the experience. It now seemed providential that, a few years ago, Sam sent her to take some classes on marketing and web design.

Before logging out, she spent some time searching out other local businesses and following their social media pages and feeds. This would help her to stay in the loop and increase her shop's visibility. Then she began inviting others to like her pages, as well, scrolling through her connections and searching for people who lived in the area. Connie was starting small, but at least it was a start.

Shortly after Connie closed her computer, a woman with short, bleach-blond hair, who looked to be in her late fifties, peeked into the store, carrying a Bromeliad plant. The woman scanned the shop, and when she spotted Connie at the table, her tired expression gave way to a bright smile.

"Hi, I'm Ruby. I've been meaning to stop by to introduce myself, but I just haven't had a spare minute all week. I own the souvenir shop next door. I just saw your social media post and thought I'd come by while we have a bit of a lull."

Connie was pleased that her social networking was already bearing fruit.

Ruby offered the Bromeliad to Connie, who accepted it gratefully and placed it on the coffee table in front of the couch, while Ginger welcomed Ruby in her own sweet way. The red plant added some additional color to the store's seating area.

"Can I get you a glass of iced tea?" Connie offered. "I brewed some fresh this morning."

"I would love one, but I'll have to make it a quick visit," she said, looking at her watch. "My sales associate will only be there a little while longer."

Connie poured tea into two ice-filled glasses, added a few leaves from one of her mint plants, and brought them to her guest. She put them on a white tray with painted hydrangeas next to a glass bowl filled with sugar packets and placed it on the coffee table in front of Ruby. She was glad to have already brought in the mint plants. They lent a homey feel to her drinks, and it was important to Connie that her store be a place where people felt welcome and enjoyed spending time, especially once she started her jewelry-making classes. She wanted her students to feel at home, as if they could stop by at any time with the questions they would undoubtedly have.

"Thank you for coming by, Ruby. It's wonderful to know I have such friendly neighbors," Connie said, handing Ruby a glass.

"Oh, it's a great little community here. We support one another," Ruby said, taking two packets of sugar from the bowl and emptying them into her iced tea. "I was glad Mickey finally got this place rented. It's a great little spot," she said, motioning to the people passing by the front window. "Despite his problems with the previous renter."

"Were there problems between Mickey and Natasha?" Connie asked.

"Well, I can't say for sure, but I did see Mickey and Natasha in a heated argument last June. I tried to keep walking and pretend I didn't hear anything, but Mickey was steaming. Something about her being late with her rent again, even though business appeared strong."

"Do you remember if there was a lot of traffic in her store during that time?"

"My souvenir shop did have a very profitable season last spring. And judging from the number of customers leaving her store with bags filled to the brim, it looked like Natasha was having a good spring, as well."

That was interesting. It was looking more and more as if business had indeed been good for Natasha. So, why had she been struggling to pay her rent?

When the women finished their iced tea, Ruby had to get back to the shop. Before leaving, she perused the Fair Trade section of the store, which was pretty much set up and ready to go.

"I love the jewelry you have. Selling Fair Trade is such a fabulous idea. Let me know how it goes. I was thinking maybe I could carry a few Fair Trade handbags in my store."

"I certainly will," Connie said, ecstatic at the possibility. "In fact, some of my artisans also make handbags, so if you are seriously interested, I could contact them about it."

"I am, but I'll let you get through your grand opening first. Then we can talk."

"Sounds like a plan. I'm so glad you stopped by. I've been meaning to visit other stores on the beach to introduce myself, but just haven't had the time. Now I'm putting it at the top of my list of priorities."

"I'd be happy to take you around some time if you'd like. Stop by when you have a chance, and we can make arrangements."

# Chapter 9

ON FRIDAY MORNING, Connie awoke before her alarm went off. After breakfast and Ginger's morning walk, she decided to take advantage of the beautiful morning and go for a short paddle along the shore before work. The salty air in her lungs and the sound of birds calling to one another as they glided through the air above the water was like a reboot for her anxious mind.

Refreshed, she stopped in the lobby for the mail on her way back upstairs and ran into Gertrude relaxing in a wingback chair and chatting with another resident. Gertrude introduced Connie to her friend, Margaret, and proceeded to tell her all about *Just Jewelry*. "I'll be at the grand opening next

Saturday," Gertrude said. "I wouldn't miss it for the world."

As Connie waited at the elevator, she couldn't help but smile when she heard Gertrude strongly encouraging Margaret to come and bring friends. With friends like Gertrude spreading the word, the grand opening was sure to be a success.

After a quick shower, Connie and Ginger headed into the store to continue getting it ready for the big day, which was quickly approaching. She went out back to put away the juicer and fresh fruit she had purchased to provide those much-needed afternoon energy boosts. She had already set up a cart in the storage room next to the refrigerator, along with her electric kettle and an assortment of tea. There was a back door next to the storage room, so she kept her mint plants on a shelf outside, where they would get plenty of sunshine. She also had a separate tiny cart for Ginger's food and treats. The shop was really starting to feel like a home away from home.

Connie couldn't resist snapping a photo of her fruit and juicer and texting it to Gallagher, along with the message: *Your healthy lifestyle is inspiring me. I even got a paddleboard last weekend.*

Gallagher responded within a few seconds. *You do me proud.*

Throughout the rest of the morning, Connie settled into a rhythm of cleaning and stocking, and at 2:00, Grace arrived unexpectedly with a picnic basket in hand.

"What are you doing here?" Connie asked. "It's your day off."

"I know, but I was finishing up some housework and figured you would be ready to stop for lunch about now, so I packed some sandwiches. I thought we could both take a break and have lunch together."

Connie gave Grace a one-armed hug, then brought the basket over to the table. "What would I do without you?"

She unpacked two turkey and swiss sandwiches with lettuce and tomato on wheat bread, some carrot sticks, two small bags of popcorn, and two cans of cranberry-lime seltzer water.

"It looks fabulous in here," Grace said, admiring the newly-stocked shelves. "You will easily be ready by next week."

"I hope so. All that's really left is to price the merchandise and continue to get the word out. I've

93

been doing everything I can to spread the word through social media and advertising. I even took out an ad in the church bulletin."

While they were eating, Connie told Grace about meeting Ruby the previous day and her offer to take them around and introduce them to some other shop owners. At Grace's insistence, they took a walk next door after lunch to see if by chance Ruby happened to be free.

"Your timing is perfect. My ace employee is working today, and she can handle the store alone for a little while," Ruby said, flashing a smile to a young woman behind the counter who was ringing up a customer.

Grace and Ruby hit it off like old friends, and Connie could barely get a word in edgewise as the two of them got acquainted. It warmed her heart to see Grace making a new friend, especially one who worked so close.

They made their way through the downtown streets, most of which ran perpendicular to the beach, following Ruby into many of the shops. There were several souvenir shops, clothing boutiques, and restaurants. If the owners were present, Ruby introduced them, and if not, Connie and Grace talked with the employees. Connie handed out the cards she had printed with information about the grand opening, and many promised to stop by before or after their shifts that day.

"We try to support one another around here, like good neighbors," Ruby said. "I think you'll find it's a nice business community to be a part of."

Ruby had strategically planned their last stop at an ice cream shop.

"I like your style," Connie said, eyeing the endless flavors of ice cream through the glass counter.

"We might as well get some ice cream," Grace said. "It would be rude not to get one, since we're already here."

"After all, it's only research, so there will be no calories," Connie said. She insisted on treating Grace and her new friend.

Spotting Ruby, a woman with dark, wavy hair and deep brown eyes, who appeared to be in her late thirties, came over from behind the counter to join them at their table.

"Emily, how are you?" Ruby asked, introducing the woman to Connie and Grace as the owner of the ice cream shop.

"Welcome to the neighborhood," Emily said. "As you can tell, *Friendly Scoops* is the coolest shop in all of downtown Sapphire Beach."

"You're certainly living the dream," Connie said. "Ice cream and the beach, what more could anyone ask for?"

Emily winked. "I see we're going to get along well."

Ruby put her arm around Emily. "All this ice cream, and she still manages to stay so thin. It's just not fair."

"It's ten percent good genes and ninety percent working my rear end off at the gym."

Emily's gaze settled on Connie as if she were trying to recall something. "Say, aren't you in the same shop where *Natasha's Boutique* used to be located?"

Connie licked her mint chocolate chip ice cream cone and nodded. "Were you friends?"

"I wouldn't say we were friends. Natasha mostly kept to herself. But she would take her little girl here for ice cream every so often. She was good friends with Gallagher McKeon, who owns the restaurant across from you, and one of his employees."

"Penelope," Connie said. "She used to work for Natasha before..."

"Yeah, that's her," Emily said before Connie could finish. "I would see Gallagher and Natasha around town a lot. I thought they were dating at first, because they seemed really familiar with one another. But I think they were just good friends."

"I didn't realize they were close. I thought they were just neighbors," Connie said. In fact, Gallagher had specifically told her they were *not* close when they talked by the beach.

"I don't mean to spread rumors or anything, just saying what I saw. There was definitely a familiarity between them. They were more than just neighbors."

Connie's heart sank. Why would Gallagher lie? She liked him a lot and didn't want him to turn out to be a bad guy. It gave Connie an uneasy feeling.

After they finished their ice cream, Ruby had to get back to her boutique, so Connie returned to her store, and Grace headed home to Palm Paradise to get her bike for a light workout.

For the rest of the afternoon, Connie couldn't shake from her mind what Emily had said about Gallagher and Natasha. What reason could Gallagher possibly have to hide the fact that they were friends?

\*\*\*

Later that afternoon when Connie got back to Palm Paradise, she took Ginger for a walk before heading upstairs. Although it was nearly April, it felt more like a July evening would have felt in Boston. As happy as she was to be wearing flip-flops in late March, she had a feeling the Floridian climate would continue to seem strange for a while.

As she and Ginger strolled down Sapphire Beach Boulevard, Connie sifted through the new information she had learned over the past few days.

Penelope hadn't seen any indication of drug use, and she spent a lot of time with Natasha. She painted a picture of Natasha as a loving mother who had devoted herself to giving her daughter a better life, which was consistent with the diary Connie had found. If Natasha didn't want her daughter living with Jordan for some reason, as Penelope had indicated, perhaps he had an ulterior motive for making Natasha look bad and fabricated her drug problem. Connie wished she knew more about what had happened between Natasha and Jordan.

Then Ruby said she had seen Mickey and Natasha in a heated argument. That didn't look good for Mickey. Maybe after hearing from Jordan that she had once done drugs, he made up the story of the drug needle to throw off the police, and then he killed Natasha. A shiver ran through her body, thinking that her landlord could be capable of that.

And what was going on with Gallagher? Why on earth would he hide his relationship with Natasha?

With no fresh leads, the police seemed to have again set aside the case, which made Connie more determined than ever to investigate. But she found herself in the same position as the police - with several suspects but not enough evidence on any of them to draw any solid conclusions.

By the time she got upstairs, it was a little after 6:00, and the sun was beginning to set. Connie fed Ginger, put some chicken in the oven for herself, and made up a salad. Then she relaxed until dinner was ready.

After a quick bite to eat, Connie went back to work stringing copper-colored satin finish beads onto the necklace she was hoping to complete soon. After making some progress, she decided to break for a cup of tea. When she glanced at the clock on the stove, she was surprised to see that a few hours had passed since she started working on the necklace. Like a conversation with a faithful friend, creating jewelry always provided Connie with a healthy diversion, especially when she needed to get her mind off things.

She finished her tea and returned to work on the necklace. Since it was Friday night, and at least until the shop opened next week, she still had the luxury of sleeping in the next morning, she decided to work as long as she could. As she continued, her thoughts drifted to Natasha's diary. She wondered about Natasha's friend Mac and the eagle. What was it about that eagle that seemed familiar?

As she wearily labored on, an image of Gallagher's tattoo suddenly flashed through her mind, as if her subconscious was putting together the pieces of a puzzle while she worked. Gallagher had a tattoo of a soaring eagle. And wasn't his last name McKeon?

Could Gallagher be Mac? The same Mac who was deeply touched that Natasha had named her daughter Victoria as a sign that she would soar above the past, like an eagle? Had they known each other before moving to Sapphire Beach? That certainly would explain Emily's impression that they were close.

She checked the time on her phone. It was 10:45, almost closing time for the restaurant. Connie grabbed her purse and raced over to *Gallagher's Tropical Shack*.

# Chapter 10

WHEN CONNIE ARRIVED at *The Shack*, most of the customers had already cleared out. There were only a few patrons left finishing up their meals or drinks.

"I'm sorry. We close at 11," the hostess said when she spotted Connie looking around the restaurant.

"I'm not here to eat. I was just looking for Gallagher. My name is Connie. I'm a friend of his."

Penelope waved as she cleared off a table near the bar.

Seeming to take that as corroboration of Connie's claim, the hostess said, "He's in his office out back. I'll tell him you're here."

She hadn't yet been inside *Gallagher's Tropical Shack*, and she really liked the vibe. Like her own shop, it had a driftwood accent wall. But the dining room had windows that stretched across three of the walls and contained pictures, vintage surfboards, and an old canoe mounted on the space above them.

Within a few minutes, Gallagher came out with a surprised look on his face.

"Hey, Connie, what brings you here this time of night?"

She took a few steps forward, so that she would be out of earshot of the hostess. "I was in the neighborhood and thought I'd stop by. How was your night, Mac?"

His jaw dropped when she called him 'Mac', confirming her suspicions.

"Can we talk somewhere in private?"

He nodded. "Let's go to my office."

She followed him to a room behind the kitchen containing a desk, a computer, and a few file cabinets. He also had a refrigerator and a cart stocked with a tub of protein powder, a box of granola bars, natural almond butter, and a large bowl of fruit.

He invited her to take a seat on a brown leather loveseat while he wheeled over his desk chair.

"Nobody's called me Mac since Natasha. How did you know?"

Connie came clean and told him about the diary that she had found and how, between the eagle reference and the nickname, she eventually put the pieces together.

"Why didn't you tell me that you knew her?"

His fidgeted in his chair. "It's times like these that I wish I could have a drink."

Connie leaned forward. "It's okay. You can trust me, Gallagher. I only want to help. Do the police know the two of you have a past?"

"Yes, of course. I told them everything I knew when she disappeared."

"Would you mind telling *me*?"

He paused and took a deep breath, as if thinking it over. Then he spoke slowly. "I first met Natasha a little over four years ago, before she even met Jordan. Right away, we hit it off well, and she became like a sister to me. I had just quit drinking after hitting rock bottom, and we were next-door neighbors in the same apartment building. I was finally getting back on my feet, managing a nearby restaurant, and she was working in retail. We had similar crazy late-night hours, so occasionally we would grab a late breakfast or run into each other at the pool and talk about our dreams. She was saving to one day open a boutique, and I wanted to own a restaurant on the beach." He crossed his arms and raised his shoulders, as if he were cold, but the air conditioning unit on the wall was turned off.

"One day she told me about a group that she went to called 'New Light.'"

"Sounds like a cult," Connie said.

"Where were you four years ago?"

Connie felt her jaw drop. "You mean it *was* a cult?"

Gallagher nodded. "Of course, we didn't see it at the time. Jordan Sugrue, a charming, smooth talker, was the leader of the group, and somehow, we slowly got sucked in. At first, he was just preaching a self-empowerment philosophy, and we were both in a vulnerable place - I was still in the early stages of recovery dealing with my own demons, and Natasha had lost both parents as a child and grew up being shuffled between foster homes. In hindsight, I think he targeted Natasha from the beginning, giving her special attention and encouragement. They started dating, and after a while, she became pregnant with Victoria. By the time the baby was born, we both realized it was a cult. Natasha connected the dots first, as Sugrue became more and more controlling, and she soon had me convinced, as well."

Connie let out a long sigh. "Is that when you left?"

"We both wanted to cut ties from the group, but Sugrue made it difficult, especially for Natasha. Once we saw through him, his whole persona fell like a house of cards." Gallagher closed his eyes and raised a clenched fist to his mouth for a moment. "We started to see him as the narcissistic manipulator that he was, but we were afraid to leave. She didn't want Victoria to be raised in that environment, but his followers were fiercely loyal, and we didn't know what they or Sugrue might do if we tried to leave. He had already made it clear that there would be serious repercussions if we tried."

Gallagher grabbed a small bottle of water from the refrigerator and offered one to Connie.

"No, thanks," she said.

He took a long sip, nearly emptying the bottle, then continued his story. "Finally, we were able to get some incriminating photos and videos of Sugrue threatening us and revealing his manipulation tactics, and we blackmailed him into giving us back all the money we had donated to his group over the eighteen months that we were involved. We swore we would take the photos and videos straight to the press if he tried to contact us or see Victoria. Then we left the Panhandle and came to Sapphire Beach. He was furious, but we left him with little choice. We convinced him that his little community would be toast if he didn't leave us alone."

When Gallagher finished, he put his face in his hands, and Connie went over to give him a hug. "You guys were so brave. Some people never make it out of those situations."

He gave her an appreciative smile as she sat back down on the couch. "I just feel so foolish. Natasha never regretted anything, because otherwise she wouldn't have had Victoria, which I guess is true. But I can't help but feel that, if I had seen through that guy faster, so much pain could have been avoided."

"So, you think Jordan is responsible for her disappearance?"

"I think it's connected with him, for sure. The local police have had their eyes on Sugrue and his group for a while now, so I'm just leaving it in their hands and trying to get on with my life." He shook his head. "How did this get so bad? Not only is Natasha gone, but now Sugrue has Victoria. It couldn't have turned out any worse."

Connie's heart tightened at seeing the pain on his face. "Gallagher, did Natasha ever have a problem with drugs?"

"No, absolutely not. Sugrue started those rumors to undermine Natasha's credibility. She was as clean as they come. In fact, she was a great support to me in the days after I gave up drinking."

The two sat in silence for a few moments.

"You know, I always had the feeling that Natasha had more evidence against Sugrue that she didn't share with me, but she never would admit to it. She insisted on keeping everything, so I don't even know where she hid it. As far as I know, it's lost forever. I wish I had it to show the police. Maybe it could somehow help them to put him behind bars."

Connie exhaled deeply. She stood up to leave and put her hand on Gallagher's shoulder. "Jordan is *not* going to win. Not only for Natasha's sake, but for Victoria's, as well."

# Chapter 11

CONNIE GRABBED HER PHONE on Saturday morning and sent a group text to Elyse and Stephanie. *Yikes! My date with Zach is tomorrow, and my grand opening is one week away. I'm officially freaking out. Anyone free for a drink tonight?*

Within a few minutes she had two responses. Stephanie's was first: *Wine and snacks at my house at 7?* And a second from Elyse: *I can make it. Emma will be at a sleepover. I'll bring the wine.*

A relieved smile spread across Connie's face as she read the responses from her friends. She texted them back. *You guys are the best. I'll bring some homemade guacamole, salsa, and corn chips.*

Connie had slept later than usual, so as soon as she got up, she took a quick shower, threw on a pair of black capris, a white V-neck t-shirt, and some flip-flops, and took Ginger for a quick walk. Then she headed into the shop to get in a few hours of work.

It was about 3:00 when Connie and Ginger returned home, so she had plenty of time before her plans with Elyse and Stephanie. With her mind still reeling from her conversation with Gallagher the night before, Connie decided to reread Natasha's diary and see if she could come up with any new angles. Maybe she would receive some fresh insight in light of the new information she had about the last few years of Natasha's life.

Connie settled onto the couch with Ginger nestled on her lap and stroked her silky coat, while she started from the beginning of the soft leather diary.

She was drawn to the section where Natasha described her favorite place to go when she needed to be alone to reflect. She remembered Penelope saying that on the night she disappeared, Natasha said she was going to her thinking spot.

Connie read Natasha's description of a bench, where, seated beneath a palm tree, she could gaze at the ocean in the distance. *Great*, Connie thought, *that could be anywhere in southwest Florida.*

Absorbed in her reading, Connie was startled by the ring of her cell phone, which she had left charging on the kitchen counter. She put the diary on the coffee table, scooped up Ginger from her lap, and checked the caller ID on her phone. It was her sister, Gianna.

Connie hit "Accept."

"Hey, Gi, how's it going?"

"Hey, Connie, doing well. Just wanted to hear the sound of your voice. I miss you."

Connie felt a twinge of guilt. She had been so busy between her sleuthing and setting up her condo and her shop that she hadn't had time to be homesick. But Gianna's voice brought it on. "I miss you guys, too. How are the twins?" Gianna had two-year-old twins, Hannah and Noah.

"I wore them out this morning at the park, so they are both napping, which is no small miracle."

"Aw, there's plenty of room here. Come down whenever you want."

They caught up on each other's lives, talking as if they lived next door. After swearing her to secrecy,

Connie even confided in her about Natasha's disappearance and how she'd been asking around.

"Another mystery in Sapphire Beach? You've got to be kidding," she said.

"Natasha had a daughter who was the same age as the twins when she disappeared." Until she said it aloud, Connie hadn't realized that Victoria had been the same age as her niece and nephew. Perhaps that was one of the reasons the little girl tugged so hard on her heartstrings.

"I can't imagine not being able to raise my babies," Gianna said, her voice choking up. "Do you think she could still be alive?"

"Even though they haven't found a body, I tend to doubt it. I just don't believe she would disappear and leave her baby behind. Unless she's being held against her will."

"You mean kidnapped?"

"I suppose that's a possibility. And it's better than the alternative. But it's been about eight months since her disappearance, so it's hard to be optimistic."

She heard Gianna sigh on the other end of the phone. "They are in my prayers, and so are you, Connie. I won't mention it to Mom and Dad, but please be careful. I want you to be there to see Hannah and Noah grow up. You can't change what happened to that young woman, as tragic as it is, so don't do anything crazy."

"I promise. Hey, isn't it my job to worry about you? After all, you're my baby sister, not the other way around. When did you take on the role of older sibling?"

"I think it was somewhere around the time you started traipsing around developing countries, leaving your family at home to worry about you."

"Oh yeah, I forgot about that," she said, teasing her little sister. "I always brought you back cool presents, though, didn't I?"

"Yes, there were cool presents involved. I'll give you that," Gianna said, laughing. "But that's okay. I like worrying about you and living vicariously through you. There's only room for one adventurous sister in the family, so lucky for Mom and Dad, I took a safer path."

"Love you. Tell the twins I miss them. I'll call tomorrow when they're awake."

"Yes, please call. They will be so excited to hear from you."

After her conversation with her sister, Connie had a light supper, then made the guacamole and salsa that she promised her friends.

When she arrived at Stephanie's bungalow, Elyse's car was already in the driveway. Stephanie led Connie through the house and out to the lanai, where Elyse was sipping white wine and making herself at home on one of the wicker chairs. Stephanie set out snacks on the coffee table and poured Connie a glass of Chardonnay, which had been chilling in an ice bucket. Potted plants of various sizes, including Bismarck and Bamboo palms, Cordyline and other tropical vegetation, dressed up the lanai, and a warm breeze carried the scent of saltwater.

"So, what's all this panic about?" Elyse asked Connie, cutting right to the chase. "You said you're ahead of schedule with the store."

"I know. I was there today, and I'm really in good shape. I think it's a combination of everything - the grand opening, wanting the store to be a success after leaving everything behind, and my date with Zach tomorrow. When I woke up this morning, it all came at me at once, and I felt completely overwhelmed."

"I remember when I quit my job in Ohio to move to Sapphire Beach," Stephanie said. "I didn't even have a job lined up yet, but I knew I needed a change. So, I just left everything and stayed with my mother while I got on my feet. It was terrifying at first, but it turned out to be the best decision I ever made. Once I got a job and knew I wanted to stay, I bought this little gem," she said, referring to her bungalow.

"With a little help from your ace realtor," Elyse added, pretending to be insulted at the omission.

"Of course," Stephanie said, gently elbowing Elyse.

Her friends' friendly banter brought a smile to Connie's face. Their friendship made the transition so much easier. "I know you guys are right. I'm not having second thoughts. It's just nerves. I'm happy to be with you both tonight. Sometimes you just need to know there are people around who are cheering you on."

"As far as Zach goes, he's a great guy," Elyse said. "The two of you will have a great time parasailing tomorrow. The worst that could happen is you'll make a good friend."

Connie had to smile. "That's true. I do like him. It's just that I haven't dated that much over the years. There was this one guy, Jeremy, when I was younger. He was my first love, and we dated during college. We even talked about marriage down the line. He was supportive of my desire to go to Africa and promised he'd wait for me, but when I returned, let's just say he didn't wait. After Jeremy, I always figured that I was better off without the constraints of a relationship, so that I could follow my dreams without worrying about my heart getting broken. Besides, I was so busy at *Feeding the Hungry* that there really wasn't time."

"Are you sure there wasn't time, or were you just scared?" Elyse asked.

Connie chuckled at Elyse's insight. "Let's just say I was less afraid when I went hiking in the Kakamega Forest in Kenya at night," Connie said.

Stephanie laughed. "I'm with Connie. We don't all meet the love of our life in high school, you know."

"You guys are so dramatic," Elyse said, rolling her eyes and laughing. "I just don't want to see Connie miss out on a great guy."

Connie looked at Elyse. "It seems that you're always pushing me to take chances. It was you who put the idea of opening a jewelry shop back into my mind to begin with in January." Connie would always remember that wonderful day when Elyse had taken her paddleboarding, then to look at a vacant shop where she pitched the idea of a jewelry shop. Elyse's instincts had been right that time, so what was she so worried about now?

"You're welcome," Elyse said, with a satisfied grin.

After enjoying the evening air a little longer, they encouraged Connie to get to bed early for her big day.

"Let me know how parasailing is," Stephanie said. "I'm thinking of giving it a try."

"Will do," Connie said as she left. "Thanks again for a great night."

# Chapter 12

THE 11:00 SUNDAY MASS was jam-packed with tourists and snowbirds, still lingering in Sapphire Beach, but Connie spotted Zach right away, seated toward the back. He turned around as if he had been looking for her. When they made eye contact, he smiled and motioned that he had been saving a seat.

They didn't have a chance to say much, since Mass was beginning, but Zach handed her a copy of the bulletin, which he had opened to Connie's ad for the grand opening.

Connie felt a surge of pride at the half-page ad, prominently placed, containing a collage of photos of the storefront and a selection of jewelry pieces, along with text noting that Connie was a parishioner and briefly describing the concept for *Just Jewelry*.

Ready or not, the grand opening was happening in less than a week.

After Mass, Zach walked Connie to her car, and they arranged to meet at Connie's condo in a half-hour. They each needed to go home to pick up their bathing suits for their lunch and parasailing date.

Zach arrived right on time, and they headed straight to a restaurant on the beach, close to Sapphire Beach Boat Rentals, where Zach had made reservations for parasailing, and got a table on the deck outside. The temperature had climbed into the mid-eighties, with the sun strong in the sky, so they requested a table in the shade and ordered two lemonades.

After they placed their order, Connie caught Zach up on her first two weeks as a resident of Sapphire Beach.

"Sounds like you're keeping busy. Even with settling into your new home, preparing for the grand opening, and purchasing a paddleboard, I hear you've still had time to ask around about Natasha's disappearance," Zach said. "You just can't stay away from a good mystery, can you?"

She was relieved that his tone was more playful than accusing. A stern lecture would not be the best way to start a first date.

"I can't help but feel a sense of connection with Natasha. We both had a dream that led us to the same shop," Connie said.

"That's an interesting way of looking at it. I suppose I should discourage you, but I doubt you'd listen. Besides, your attitude is refreshing. Most people don't want to get involved in other people's business. You know, 'I'm not my brother's keeper' and all."

"I never thought of it that way," Connie said.

"That's one of the things I admire about you." His gaze was intense, as if he were studying her. "It's probably what drew you into humanitarian work. You take others' concerns upon yourself as if they are your own."

Connie chuckled. He had her number.

"Some call it concern for neighbor," she said, "and others call it meddling."

He laughed. "I guess it's a matter of perspective. But I admire that you spent time volunteering after college, and that you were so moved by what you saw that you dedicated your life to serving others."

Connie had forgotten that she had shared so much with him when they had taken a walk together back in January. Elyse had been encouraging her to consider opening a jewelry shop, but Connie was torn, because, as much as she loved Sapphire Beach, she wasn't sure she was ready to leave her work with *Feeding the Hungry*. Connie was pleasantly surprised that he had been paying such close attention.

"When we talked a few months ago," Zach said, "I was hoping you would end up staying in Sapphire Beach, but I respected your commitment to your work."

Connie took another sip of lemonade. "I prayed and thought a lot about it, and when the idea of selling Fair Trade jewelry came to me, I was so excited. I just knew it was the right thing. I'm hoping that, as time goes on, I can dedicate more and more of the store to Fair Trade. While I still need to make a living, inheriting my aunt Concetta's condo put me in a position to fulfill this dream. In that sense, it's as much her shop as mine. Both the store and the condo are a constant reminder of her love for me."

"I'm sure you will do her proud," he said, holding her gaze. "I, for one, will purchase gifts at *Just Jewelry* for my female relatives and encourage my friends to do the same," he said, as the server arrived with their food.

Zach had ordered a grouper sandwich with fries, but Connie was afraid to eat anything heavy before parasailing, so she kept it light with a grilled chicken Caesar salad.

Zach reached across the table and took her hand while they said a quick blessing before they dug into their meals.

"I understand your dilemma about which way to follow your heart," Zach said. "Before I became a cop, I considered becoming a priest. My uncle is a priest, and he spent a lot of time with our family while I was growing up. I was really torn for a while."

Connie almost choked on her salad at his revelation. "Wow! What changed your mind?" she asked.

"Well, kind of like you, I prayed and thought about it. The way I saw it, they were both ways to serve God, but I couldn't do both, so I just had to discern which way He was calling me. In hindsight, I know I made the right choice."

"I haven't known you for long," Connie said, "but being a detective seems like the perfect fit. You have a lot of insight into what makes people tick and a strong desire to see justice served."

He smiled thoughtfully and thanked her for the compliment.

As they finished their meal, the conversation drifted back toward the case.

"I keep going down false paths," Connie said. "I even kind of suspected poor Gallagher the other night."

"Gallagher McKeon, the restaurant owner?" he asked with a smirk.

"Yes. It turns out that Gallagher and Natasha were old friends, from before Sapphire Beach." She didn't mention how she discovered that, unsure of whether she should admit to snapping pictures of Natasha's diary.

"That's right. They were both tangled up in Jordan Sugrue's cult up in the Panhandle. I went up to interview him after Natasha's disappearance. That place gives me the creeps."

"Do you think he's involved in her disappearance?" Then she realized he couldn't directly discuss the case. "Sorry, I forgot," she said.

"Let's just say I can see why Natasha and Gallagher wanted to get out of there."

Connie's heart broke for Victoria. That little girl was one of the main reasons Connie couldn't believe Natasha would have run away. She would never have fought so hard to leave, only to do something that would cause Victoria to have to return to her father. The words of the diary came back to Connie: *I named my daughter Victoria to symbolize that my child would be victorious over the past.*

While their server was getting the check, Connie pointed up at the parasailers. "I can't wait," she said.

When they finished their lemonades, they headed to a nearby public restroom to change into bathing suits. Then they walked across the sugar-white sand to Sapphire Beach Boat Rentals, where Connie received a warm greeting from Ashley and Travis, who were ready for them, since Zach had called ahead for reservations.

There were eight other people coming out with them - two groups of three friends and another couple. Parasailers had the option of going up alone or in groups of two or three.

When everyone had arrived, they hopped into the speedboat, and Travis motored them about fifteen hundred feet away from the shore. Connie and Zach volunteered to go up first, so after a quick tutorial, he fitted them each with a safety harness, and they waited side by side in a seated position, as the sail gently lifted them up off the boat until they were floating high above the Gulf of Mexico.

Once they reached what Zach jokingly called cruising altitude, a group of seagulls flew beneath them.

Connie looked over at Zach, who was wearing a broad smile. "This is amazing," she said, leaning back into the blue sky.

Zach nodded and pointed to a dolphin gliding across the waters below.

After a few minutes, Travis skillfully brought them low enough for their feet to dip into the water, then they rose back up, and the world below became small once again as tiny sunbathers and umbrellas colorfully dotted the coastline.

As the boat motored along, Connie's gaze drifted off into the distance. From her unique vantage point, she could see all of Sapphire Beach - Palm Paradise, the pier, the downtown shops. She even thought she spotted Stephanie's bungalow.

Connie looked further into the distance toward Sapphire Beach State Park. The grass, palm trees, and areas of wild vegetation overlooking little inlets of seawater was truly breathtaking, reminding her that she hadn't taken a walk through the park since she returned.

Suddenly, her eyes were drawn to a specific spot in the park, as if something in her subconscious had pulled her attention there. An entry in Natasha's diary, which she had read the night before, flashed into Connie's mind.

Natasha wrote that her favorite spot, the one where, according to Penelope, she had gone to think the night she disappeared, consisted of a bench on the grass under a palm tree where she had a view of the water. The first time Connie read that passage, she imagined it could be anywhere in southwest Florida, but as she looked down at the park with her unique bird's eye view, something clicked. Natasha's thinking spot had to be in the state park.

Connie's heart raced at the realization. Could she be right? There was nothing she could do five hundred feet above the Gulf of Mexico. Besides, she didn't want to ruin Zach's experience, so there was no point in mentioning it until they were on solid ground.

She tried to put the idea out of her mind until she landed, but it was a struggle. She spent the last few minutes in the air willing herself to enjoy the scenery and the company. Finally, their time in the sky neared its end, and the tiny boat below, which looked like a toy floating on a vast ocean, grew larger as they slowly descended toward the water. Connie had her doubts as to whether Travis would be able to guide them onto the landing deck of the boat, but sure enough, they touched down in the same seated position as when they took off, all limbs intact.

It seemed like an eternity as they waited for the three other groups to have their turn. Connie and Zach recounted their favorite parts of the experience, while she relished the feel of the salty air pushing back her hair as the boat motored along the coastline.

Even though she had been anxious to get back and tell Zach what she had discovered, when the boat returned to the beach, she also hated to see it end.

"That was amazing, Zach," she said, giving him a slight hug.

He looked pleased that she had enjoyed herself so much. "It was better than I even imagined. Thanks for sharing it with me," he said. "Would you like to go for a walk along the beach?"

"Normally I would, but there's something I have to tell you - something I saw up there."

He gave her a puzzled look. "Okay."

Connie recapped the description in the diary of Natasha's favorite spot, coming clean about having snapped pictures of it when she found it, and how Penelope said Natasha had gone off to think the night she disappeared. "At first, I thought it could literally be anywhere in the area, but the more I think about it, there aren't a ton of spots that fit her exact description. Since Natasha had described her thinking spot as secluded, we know it couldn't be anywhere along Sapphire Beach Boulevard, which is the only street that runs along the Gulf," she said. "And if she was killed in the park, it would have to be a secluded spot. After floating above the town for fifteen minutes, I think I have an idea where it must be."

Zach followed Connie's eyes towards the direction of the park. "You think she could be buried somewhere in Sapphire Beach State Park?"

Connie stared at the ground and let out a sigh. "I hope not. I'd rather her be found alive somewhere, but it's worth taking a ride to check it out."

After changing out of their bathing suits and meeting back up at Zach's Jeep a few minutes later, they drove through the downtown area and followed the coastline to Sapphire Beach State Park.

# Chapter 13

LEAVING ZACH'S CAR at the entrance, they headed on foot toward the path that meandered around the ocean side of the park. It was only a half-mile or so in length, and there were only a handful of spots that matched Natasha's description.

After several fruitless searches, they came upon one final possibility. Zach went to explore one of the clusters of wild vegetation, while Connie sat on the bench and scanned the area around her.

She wandered across the grass over to an area of bushes and followed it to the other side, which was not visible from the main path. She walked around its perimeter, scrutinizing the ground beneath her and looking for any sign that the earth had been disturbed. Zach had assured her that, even ten months later, there would likely be some signs of disturbance.

On the far side of the shrubs was a tiny mound of dirt, barely perceptible, as if someone had dug a whole and left a remnant of the pile of dirt. Next to it, the dirt was a tiny bit lower than the rest of the ground.

"Zach, can you check this out?"

He came over and examined the area closely. "I'm calling this in."

Within fifteen minutes, Sergeant Donovan and Josh were there. Shortly after they arrived, they called in a team of forensic archaeologists to dig up the area.

Connie slipped over to a bench a short distance away when the forensic archaeologists arrived. As she looked out at the horizon, she wondered if Natasha's last moments had been in that very spot.

It was evident why Natasha might have loved it there. A majestic Christmas palm stood like a protective friend a few yards away from the bench, and its branches swayed in the soft sea breeze against a backdrop of endless blue and green.

If that was indeed the last place that Natasha had been alive, Connie hoped she didn't see anything coming or have the time to realize that her daughter might end up back in the life that she had fought so hard to free her from. Connie prayed that the peace surrounding that spot had enveloped Natasha's soul during the last moments of her life.

Connie jumped when Zach came up beside her and took a seat. She didn't realize she had been lost in thought.

"Are you okay?" he asked. "I mean, all things considered."

Connie shrugged. "Part of me is hoping I was wrong to bring you here, and she is still alive somewhere. But then another part of me feels that there is no way she could possibly be alive, and I'm just hoping that we have finally found her body so she can receive a proper burial."

Zach draped his arm around her, and she rested her head on his shoulder. "This is not how I imagined our date would end," he said softly, with a regretful smile. "I wanted everything to go just right."

"I don't know. If you ignore the potential crime scene, the police cars, and the forensic archaeologists just off to the side, this *is* the perfect end to a first date."

He smiled gratefully. "At least let me take you home. These guys are going to be a while," he said, "so there's no point in waiting around. It's a painstaking process that involves lots of pictures, slow digging, and careful assessment."

"Okay, thanks. I should probably get home to feed Ginger, anyway."

They walked the half-mile back to Zach's Jeep in relative silence; then he drove her back to Palm Paradise and walked her upstairs.

"I enjoyed our conversation at lunch," she said. "And parasailing was incredible."

"Well, I hope you'll let me take you out again. You know, so we can get the ending right."

Connie laughed. "I'd like that."

They agreed that he would call her after the grand opening, which was only six days away, to make plans for another date. "I'll be sure to stop by on Saturday, too," he said. Then he leaned down and kissed her cheek. She was glad to have been with Zach when she had her realization about Natasha earlier, not simply because he was a detective, but also because he had a quiet strength that brought her comfort.

"Thanks. I could use the moral support. And please let me know what happens with the excavation."

"I will. I'm heading back there now."

After Zach left, Connie stepped into the shower, hoping that the warm water would wash away her sadness along with the salt and sand, but no such luck.

Feeling as though she were operating on autopilot, she fed Ginger and took her out. When she got back upstairs, she slipped into some comfy pajamas. The DVR indicated that it was after 6:00, and she realized she hadn't eaten dinner. With no ambition to cook, she heated up a frozen meal, which she kept on hand for just such times, and a big mug of herbal tea and curled up on the couch. Although it was seventy-six degrees in the condo, the past couple of hours left her feeling chilled.

Connie decided not to tell Gallagher or Penelope about what she and Zach had discovered in case it was a false alarm, but she needed to talk to someone, so she grabbed her phone from her purse and called Elyse.

"So, how was your date?" she answered, without bothering to say hello.

"Let's just say it was memorable." Connie told Elyse the entire story, starting with her conversation with Gallagher on Friday night, since they hadn't discussed the case at Stephanie's the night before, and ending with her date with Zach and their post-parasailing discovery.

"Wow! All this happened in two days? There's never a dull moment with you, is there?" Elyse said laughing. "I can't believe you actually figured out where Natasha might be buried while parasailing. That's unreal."

"Zach dropped me off a few minutes ago and said he was going back to the excavation site. I'm just here, hanging tight and saying a few prayers."

"So, are you going to see Zach again?"

"He's going to call me after the grand opening to make plans for a second date."

Elyse let out a squeal. "I knew you two would hit it off."

"We really do have a lot in common. He seems like a solid guy. And, of course, parasailing was the best. It was such a rush being so high above the Gulf Coast and seeing the whole town in a glance."

"Floating on air with a handsome guy by your side. Sounds like the perfect first date."

Connie had to agree. "Thank you for encouraging me to go out with him. Your friendship means a lot to me."

"The feeling is mutual, Connie. I'm so happy to have you in my life, and in Emma's, too."

\*\*\*

At 9:30 PM, Connie received a text from Zach. *Is it too late to stop by?*

*Come on over,* she replied.

Within fifteen minutes, Zach was sitting in her living room. She could tell by the solemn expression on his face that the news wasn't good.

"They found a body, and it appears to be Natasha's."

Tears stung the back of Connie's eyes. Even though she had never met Natasha, she felt like they were friends. She didn't expect the loss to hit her so personally, but it did.

After a period of silence, Zach said, "Although there hasn't been time for DNA testing, the body had the same hair as Natasha and was wearing the same clothes that she was described as wearing the night she disappeared. There was also a mini-wallet in her pocket with her driver's license and a few credit cards. It will probably all be on the late news tonight, so I wanted to come by and tell you in person."

"Are you any closer to discovering who did this?"

Zach shook his head. "She was shot in the back of the head and then buried. She probably never knew what hit her. It's officially a murder investigation now."

"Poor Victoria."

Zach looked at her with a half-smile. "Ironically, it's Victoria who helped us to ID her."

Connie shot him a confused look.

"Apparently the baby liked to grab her mother's phone and take pictures, and that's what she did the night of her mother's disappearance. Thanks to Victoria, we have a bunch of pictures of Natasha the night she disappeared, which gave us additional confirmation on her clothes and that she was wearing her hair in a ponytail that night."

"I hope you'll investigate Jordan Sugrue and his little group. From what Gallagher told me, he is a dangerous man."

"We'll be exploring every possible lead and going back to talk to people again in light of this new information. Josh is over at Gallagher's right now, letting him and Penelope know, since they were closest to her. He didn't want them hearing about it on the news."

Despite a long day, by the time Zach left, Connie was so wound up that she couldn't sleep. Rather than lying in bed and staring at the ceiling, she took her laptop over to the couch and did an internet search for "Jordan Sugrue, New Light Community."

Within seconds his picture popped up, and she was looking him in the eyes through her computer screen. Chills ran down her spine. He was good looking, if you liked men with shoulder-length hair and dark, penetrating eyes. He looked to be in his late thirties, probably about ten years older than Natasha. His hair was combed back, and his expression was confident. He struck Connie as someone who had a lot of charisma. Too bad he insisted on using his God-given gifts for such evil.

Connie had the urge to close her computer. It was downright creepy having him in her living room, even if it was just his picture. But she resisted and clicked on a few links. She quickly discovered that Jordan was the author of several books. She went over to his website to check out some of them. As she read through the book descriptions, it seemed like he was basically selling the same propaganda packaged in slightly different ways, talking about his philosophy of self-empowerment and inviting people to learn more about his group.

According to his website, he and his followers gathered regularly at a meeting space in a remote location in Florida's Panhandle, and everyone who "felt the calling" was invited to check them out. Apparently, there were people from around the country who had decided to relocate to be closer to like-minded people.

Jordan's demeanor reminded her of a sociology professor with boundary issues whom she once had in college. Connie had always avoided him, but she later heard rumors of his inappropriate relationships with students.

In her explorations, Connie also came across numerous photos of Jordan speaking to large crowds at both indoor and outdoor venues. One photo was taken of Jordan from the back, facing the crowd. His listeners appeared spellbound as he spoke.

Connie stared for a moment at the faces of two of the women in the front row who looked familiar, but she couldn't place them.

She could imagine Jordan sweeping in with sweet talk and making Natasha and Gallagher feel special during a vulnerable time in their lives, offering them a place with him and his followers. She grew angry as she thought of this man taking advantage of Natasha to the point where she became pregnant, and then giving her and Gallagher a hard time about leaving.

Connie's heart ached, and whether or not Jordan Sugrue was involved in Natasha's murder, this guy had to be stopped.

# Chapter 14

ON MONDAY MORNING, although her heart still felt heavy, Connie tried her best to refocus on her preparations for the grand opening, despite everything that happened the night before.

After a couple of hours of pricing jewelry, Connie and Grace took a mid-morning break and settled onto the sofa, each with a cup of steaming tea. The temperature outside was climbing into the eighties, but it still felt soothing to wrap her hands around a warm mug. Apparently, you could take the girl out of the Northeast, but you couldn't take the Northeast out of the girl.

As they planned the rest of the day, Connie noticed Gallagher and Penelope somberly making their way across the street.

"Those poor kids," Grace said. "They look devastated." First thing that morning, Connie had filled Grace in on what happened the night before.

Connie and Grace got up to greet them at the door, and they both gave each of them a long hug.

"I'm so sorry about what happened to Natasha," Connie said. "I was hoping things would turn out differently."

Gallagher and Penelope followed Connie to the seating area while Grace poured two more cups of tea with the water in the electric kettle, which was still hot.

"How are you two doing?" Connie asked. "I know Detective Miller came by the restaurant last night to give you the news."

Tears streamed down Penelope's face, and Grace fished out a package of tissue from her purse. She handed one to Penelope and placed the package down on the coffee table.

"Thank you," she managed.

"The police said that you led them to the body," Gallagher said to Connie. "How on earth did you figure out where she was?"

Connie pushed her dark hair out of her eyes. "It was a combination of the details Natasha wrote in her diary about her favorite thinking spot, and the fact that Penelope was babysitting Victoria on the night of Natasha's disappearance so that she could get away and think," Connie said. "Yesterday I went parasailing, and, while looking down onto the Sapphire Beach from so high above, I saw the park, and it just clicked. I happened to be with Detective Zachary Hughes and told him about my suspicions. We went over to check it out, and you know the rest."

At the mention of Zach's name, Grace gave Connie an inquisitive look. Connie had neglected to mention that she was with Zach on Sunday afternoon when she made her discovery. She wasn't trying to hide anything, but that detail didn't seem important in light of all that had happened.

Connie looked away to avoid eye contact but knew she would have to tell Grace all about it after Gallagher and Penelope left.

"As much as I was hoping that it would turn out differently with Natasha, at least this gives us some closure. We now know that she is not alive somewhere trying to escape from kidnappers," Penelope said.

Gallagher let out a long sigh. "I, for one, will feel better when the killer is behind bars. "At least now it's officially a murder investigation."

"I was on Jordan Sugrue's website last night trying to get a feel for what he's all about," Connie said. "That man is beyond creepy. I hope the police will be investigating him and his group."

"So do I," Gallagher said. "Besides Sugrue, Natasha didn't have any enemies that I know of, so I can't imagine anyone else being behind it. The guy's as slick as a snake, so he even could have had someone else in his group do it. He's always testing their loyalty. He'll be hard to pin down."

"He's obviously a very dangerous and unstable man," Grace said. Then, looking directly at Connie she said, "Promise me you'll let the police handle this one."

Gallagher shot Connie a questioning glance. "*This* one?"

"Connie helped the police solve two murder cases back in January," Grace said, "and nearly got herself killed in the process."

The corners of Gallagher's mouth turned slightly upward, and he raised his eyebrows at Connie. "I'm impressed."

"Don't encourage her," Grace said.

"I know you're worried, Grace," Connie said. "I won't do anything foolish."

Grace's expression betrayed her skepticism. "Famous last words."

"Grace is right," Gallagher said. "Sugrue is out of your league. Look at what happened to Natasha."

After Gallagher and Penelope pulled themselves together, they returned to *The Shack* to finishing preparing for the lunch crowd, while Connie filled Grace in on what had been going on with Zach.

"I always liked that young man," Grace said. "And I think Concetta would like him as well."

A smile spread across Connie's face. Grace was a living connection to her Aunt Concetta and one of the many reasons Connie treasured her presence in her life.

"You do know we're both in our mid-thirties, Grace. He's hardly a *young* man."

Grace waved Connie off with a chuckle. "It's all relative, sweetie." Grace was in her mid-sixties, about the same age as her Aunt Concetta had been when she passed away last year.

After Connie filled Grace in on her date with Zach, the women got back to pricing jewelry. A few hours later they stepped back to admire their work.

"I can't believe *Just Jewelry* is finally becoming a reality," Connie said. She thought she'd be rushing around with so much more work to get done at this point, so she was pleasantly surprised at the progress as she surveyed the store.

While Connie was straightening a gold mirror on the wall, the door chimed behind her. She could see from the reflection that it was Mickey Miranda.

"It looks like you're almost ready for Saturday," he said.

"Just about," she said, meeting him across the floor. "We just have a little more pricing to do, but we're in good shape."

"I wish you all the best. I actually stopped by, because I heard on the news that Natasha's body was discovered. I just wanted to make sure you knew."

"Not only has she heard the news," Grace said, "but she also was the one who lead the police to the body."

Connie shot Grace a sharp look. She still had her suspicions about Mickey, especially since she learned from Ruby that he and Natasha had a heated discussion about the rent money, and she didn't want him to know she had been involved in finding the body.

"What do you mean?" Mickey asked. "How did you know where the body was?"

"I didn't. I just had a theory based on something Penelope said. It was a lucky guess." She looked directly into Mickey's eyes. "Now that the police know it was murder, I'm sure they'll have the killer behind bars in no time."

Mickey coughed, and his face turned as white as sea foam. "I'm sure they will. I just wanted to make sure you were okay," he managed to say, as he abruptly left the store.

Connie tried to catch up with him, but he was too far down the street by the time she got to the door.

"That was strange," Connie said. The dramatic reaction didn't make sense. Mickey and Natasha hadn't been close, so why would he behave like a grieving father? Or was his reaction the sign of a guilty conscience?

Grace shrugged her shoulders. "You never know with people. Maybe he hoped she was still alive."

"Or maybe he didn't want to talk about it, because he's guilty and afraid of being caught now that the police are investigating for murder."

"Let's hope not," Grace said. "But whatever the case, the police are handling it. We have enough work to do in this store without stopping to speculate on Mickey's behavior."

They continued to work into the early evening. When Grace left for the day, Connie grabbed Ginger's leash to take her for a leisurely walk around town. She had been cooped up all day in the shop and was looking forward to some fresh air.

As they meandered down various streets, Connie peeked in the shop windows while Ginger sniffed to her heart's content. Window shopping was a welcome distraction, but eventually the events of the previous evening pushed their way back into her mind, and she couldn't help but wonder what happened to poor Natasha.

Although Jordan was a strong suspect in Connie's mind, there were still other pieces of the puzzle to consider.

She still didn't know why Natasha's accounting ledger indicated that she was making a healthy profit, while Tracy maintained that *Natasha's Boutique* wasn't earning enough money. Connie hadn't ruled out the possibility that Tracy was connected to her murder. The fact that Natasha felt the need to keep her own records and hide them under the floorboards seemed to indicate that she had her suspicions, as well.

And, as much as she hated the idea of her landlord being involved, why did Mickey act so strangely whenever the subject of Natasha came up? Ruby had overheard a conversation where Mickey was angrily yelling at Natasha about being late with the rent. She even said that Mickey clearly wanted her out. But if there was a steady stream of customers in Natasha's shop, as Ruby had indicated, it didn't make sense that Natasha was having money problems.

However, the more important question was whether her apparent money problems were connected to her death.

# Chapter 15

EARLY TUESDAY MORNING, the ringtone of Connie's cell phone woke her from a sound sleep. Blurry eyed, she slapped her hand around her nightstand until she located her phone. The caller ID informed her that it was her landlord.

She caught a glimpse of the darkness outside through a crack in the blinds. What in the world did Mickey want so early? She balanced herself on one elbow as she held the phone to her ear with her free hand.

"Hello?"

"Hi, Connie, Mickey Miranda here."

"Hi, Mickey. Not everyone's awake at 6:00 AM to go fishing, you know. Is everything okay?"

"Not exactly. I was passing your shop this morning on my way to the pier, and the window is smashed. It looks like someone broke in. Could you meet me at your shop as soon as possible?"

The adrenaline pumping through Connie's body woke her up quicker than a shot of espresso. "Be right there," she said, tossing the phone into her purse and pulling on some clothes.

Connie scratched the top of Ginger's head while she quickly fastened her leash. "Your breakfast will have to wait until we get into the shop."

Downtown Sapphire Beach was only a mile from Palm Paradise, but her pounding heart and racing thoughts made it feel like ten. Preparing the shop for the grand opening had been going so smoothly up until now. The last thing she needed was a setback.

 She pulled up to the shop and found Mickey pacing the sidewalk and with his fishing pole leaning against the building. Her heart sank when she saw the shattered window next to the front door.

The street was deserted at that hour, so she was able to park in front of the store with no problem.

"I don't have a key with me, so I don't know the extent of the damage," Mickey said, "but I saw the broken window as I was walking by on my way fishing."

When they entered the shop, Connie's mouth went dry. Papers were strewn everywhere, as if someone had been looking for something, and movable shelving had been pushed aside. She moved through the store, closely examining the damage and checking for missing jewelry. Much of her jewelry took significant time to create, sometimes up to forty hours for one necklace, so if too much of her inventory was missing, she would likely have to postpone the grand opening.

First, she checked the Fair Trade section, which would be the hardest product to replace. She would have to get word to her artisans of what she needed, and then she would have to wait while they created new pieces and shipped them to Florida. All of her advertising had highlighted her Fair Trade products, so it would be a disaster if those were missing.

She scrutinized each jewelry display, and when she was satisfied that it was all there, she let out a long sigh of relief. Then she examined the rest of the store.

"As far I can tell, whoever broke in didn't take any jewelry," she said to Mickey, who had been following closely behind her, visibly upset.

Next, they went out back to the storeroom where several of the large shelving units had been pulled away from the wall on the right-hand side, which had a fresh basketball-sized hole in it.

"None of my inventory is missing back here, either," Connie said as she perused the shelves and opened a few containers. "It looks like someone was searching for something specific," Connie said, wondering if they found it.

Connie gave the store another inspection. She was pretty sure nothing was missing, and the damage was relatively minimal. None of the shelves or displays were damaged, so all she would have to do was push the them back into place, rearrange some of the jewelry that had fallen, and reorganize the papers that had been scattered across the floor. The only real property damage was the hole in the wall out back and the broken window. She should easily be able to get those fixed before Saturday.

Connie texted Zach to let him know what happened. He instructed her not to touch anything else and promised he'd be right over.

"I'm so sorry this happened to you, Connie," Mickey said. He looked more shaken than she felt.

Within ten minutes, Zach arrived, and she filled him in.

"Do you have any idea what they could have been looking for?" Zach asked.

Connie ran her hands through her hair. "The shop is stocked with jewelry, and the intruder didn't take any of it. There's no cash in the register yet, but it doesn't even look as though they tried to open it. Maybe someone got scared now that Natasha's disappearance is officially a murder investigation and was searching for some type of evidence in the shop that could incriminate them." She remembered how Gallagher told her that Natasha had some evidence against Jordan.

Mickey's hand trembled as he placed it on Connie's shoulder. Either he was a good actor, or he was genuinely more shaken up than Connie. "I'll find something to cover this window, and we'll get it replaced as soon as possible."

"You should go ahead and install a security system ASAP," Zach said. He put both hands on her shoulders. "And promise me you won't stay in here alone after dark until we figure out who did this."

Connie nodded. "I'll call about the alarm system this morning. I've been researching them, so I know which one I want already. It's just a matter of getting it done."

Zach called for crime scene technicians, and they spent the next couple of hours processing the store but were unable to find fingerprints or anything that might provide a clue as to the intruder's identity. After taking statements from both Connie and Mickey, Zach left. Mickey stayed behind to help Connie clean the broken glass and cover the window.

After Mickey left, Connie took her patient dog for a quick walk and filled her food and water bowls. She was glad that Grace wasn't coming in until the afternoon so that she could have everything back in place by the time she arrived, except, of course, for the hole out back and the broken window.

While Ginger was eating, Connie called about getting a security system installed and was able to convince the company to come later that day.

As Connie went about putting everything back in order, she had an uneasy feeling in the pit of her stomach. Although there was no major damage, she couldn't help but feel that her privacy had been violated and her dream threatened. She felt firsthand the fragility of even the best-laid plans.

Once the store was back in order, Connie took some more photos of her inventory and uploaded the best ones onto her social media sites to keep the buzz going about the grand opening. She also created a couple of social media ads, targeting women who lived in Sapphire Beach.

As she was sitting on the sofa and uploading the photos, she glanced out the window and saw Gallagher resolutely marching over from his restaurant.

"I just noticed your broken window," he said, as soon as he came through the door. "Is everything all right?"

Connie motioned for Gallagher to join her on the couch, and she explained what happened.

He leaned back and shook his head. "It has to be Sugrue."

"I was thinking the same thing. Now that the police know Natasha was murdered, he's probably looking for the evidence you two had against him. If he killed her and that was his motive, he probably wants to get it back now more than ever."

"Unfortunately, Natasha never told me where she hid the evidence, so I have no idea if it's even in the store or not." Gallagher smiled, but his eyes still appeared angry. "You know, part of me is glad to think that Jordan might be sweating it out. But my more practical side just wants him to stay far away from Sapphire Beach. It gives me the creeps to think that he may have been right on this street last night."

"The police told me they would patrol the neighborhood during the night. They know about your connection to Sugrue, so I'm sure they'll keep an eye on your restaurant, too."

Just as Gallagher was getting up to leave, the door opened to reveal a worried Elyse making a beeline for Connie. Emma was following behind, bouncing a volleyball.

Elyse hugged Connie, then looked around the store with surveying eyes. "Emma had a half-day at school today because of a teachers' meeting so we were playing volleyball on the beach. Josh just stopped by and told us there was a break-in last night. I don't like this one bit, Connie. Are you okay?"

Connie had to laugh at seeing Elyse more concerned than even she had been. Seeing how much her friend cared somehow made Connie feel better.

"I'm fine, Elyse, I promise. Nothing was taken, and I've already straightened up the shop. This afternoon I have a guy coming to install a security system and a glass company coming to repair the window." As she was talking, she realized that Gallagher and Elyse had never met. "By the way, this is Gallagher. He owns *Gallagher's Tropical Shack*," Connie said, pointing across the street.

Emma stopped bouncing her ball. "The restaurant with the surfboards on the wall?" Emma asked. "I love that place."

Gallagher smiled at Emma. "That's the one. I'll tell you what. Next time you come, ask for me, and I'll give you one of my super smoothies on the house. Guaranteed to give you all the energy you need to become a beach volleyball champ," he said with a wink.

Emma's face lit up. "I definitely will, thank you."

"Stay for a little while. I'll brew us some iced tea," Connie said. "I was just taking a break, anyway."

"Can I look at the jewelry?" Emma asked.

"Of course, sweetheart," Connie said.

While the tea bags were steeping, she could hear Emma bouncing the volleyball against the wall. She peeked out to the front of the store to discover she was throwing it against the driftwood accent wall, right above her jewelry. She was about to ask her to stop when she heard Elyse's irritated voice.

"Emma, you know better than that. Please stop bouncing that ball inside." Then she said to Gallagher, "She's obsessed. She can't put that ball down."

Connie brought over a tray with the iced tea and sugar. As she sat on one of the armchairs facing the accent wall, she noticed one of the pieces of wood dislodged. Without saying a word, she grabbed her ladder from out back and went up to check it out.

Elyse put a firm hand on Emma's shoulder. "I'm so sorry, Connie. Emma will pay to have that repaired from her allowance."

"It's not that," Connie said. As she pulled away a loose board, it was like deja vu. What was it with loose boards and her shop? When she pulled away the piece of driftwood from the wall, it revealed a small hole in the drywall behind it, smaller than the piece of wood. She stuck her hand inside and reached around until she discovered an envelope nailed to the wall frame.

She yanked it out and descended the ladder.

# Chapter 16

GALLAGHER SHOT UP from his seat to see what Connie had found. He eagerly took the envelope and brought it to the coffee table, ripping it open and dumping out its contents. Out poured a stack of photos wrapped in an elastic band, a flash drive, and a key.

"Great job, Emma," he said.

Elyse gave Gallagher a menacing look. She did not seem happy that he was praising Emma's carelessness.

Connie flipped through the stack of photos, all of which contained an angry Jordan Sugrue who appeared to be losing his temper with various people.

"Helloooo, Brother Jordan," Gallagher said. "This is the side of him we came to know and *not* love in the New Light Community."

"*Brother* Jordan?" Connie inquired.

"That's what he insisted we all call him."

The photos revealed a man who was a far cry from the peaceful and self-assured leader that was portrayed all over the Internet.

Connie studied the photos. There were several of the same faces that she saw when she researched him online, sitting in the front row, captivated as he delivered his speeches. Two of the women in particular still looked familiar. She wracked her brain as she stared at them but could not place them. She brought them to Gallagher's attention. Although they looked familiar, he didn't know the names of those two women.

"I just can't believe these people couldn't see through his charade," Connie said. "Why didn't they just leave when they saw him acting this way?"

Gallagher shrugged. "It's hard to explain if you've never experienced something like that. He's a master at exploiting peoples' weaknesses and vulnerabilities. Whatever perceived benefit his members are receiving from the group must be enough to keep them there."

After they flipped through the photos, Connie got her laptop and plugged in the flash drive. It contained several audio files, so she clicked on the first one. Nausea came over her as the sound of Jordan Sugrue's voice came booming from her speakers. His voice filled the store like an unwelcome guest.

"Jackpot," Gallagher said. "These are the files we used to break free from New Light."

Like the photos, the videos revealed a Jordan Sugrue who was controlling, demanding, and narcissistic. He expressed the high expectations he held for his followers, repeatedly using words like 'family' and 'loyalty' to disguise his selfish demands.

When they had heard enough, Elyse called Josh, and he came right over along with Zach, who made his second trip to the store that morning.

As soon as they arrived, Emma ran up to Josh, her blond ponytail bouncing from side to side on her back. "Dad, I found some key evidence and broke the case wide open."

"Is that right?" he said, glancing at Elyse.

169

"Yes, your daughter and her volleyball," Elyse said.

"It looks like we have a regular Nancy Drew on our hands," Zach said. "If professional beach volleyball doesn't work out, maybe she can follow in her old man's footsteps."

After Connie showed Josh and Zach where she found the envelope, Gallagher explained the significance of the photos and audio files, and how he and Natasha had used them to extricate themselves from Sugrue's community.

"This must have been what he was looking for when he broke in last night," Gallagher said. "Now I'm more convinced than ever that it had to be him."

"I have to agree," Connie said. "Nothing was stolen last night, and the intruder left a hole in the wall in my storeroom. I'd say the odds are good that he was looking for this envelope."

Connie picked up the key that they had found along with the other items and held it up. "You never told us what this was for, Gallagher."

"That's because I've never seen it before. The photos and audio files are the only evidence we had against Sugrue. But, as I said before, I always had a gut feeling that Natasha had more information than she shared with me. It's possible that she had evidence even I didn't know about."

"I don't understand why she wouldn't tell you?" Connie asked. "It seemed like you were a team."

"She may have wanted to protect me. We worked together to obtain the photos and audio files, but she was obviously closer to Jordan than I was. She may have taken something else without telling me, as added insurance. She was always more fearful of him than I was, since she had Victoria to worry about, too."

Zach took a closer look at the small key with a rounded bow. "It could be a safety deposit box key or a key to a padlock. We'll look into it."

After the police left, Elyse and Emma stayed behind to keep Connie company until the installer from the security company arrived. Gallagher was shorthanded and had to prepare for the lunch rush, and nobody seemed to want Connie to be alone in the shop.

Before leaving, he refastened the board to the wall for Connie, in case Steve or Brittany couldn't make it back before the grand opening.

Connie insisted that she felt perfectly safe, since it was late morning and the downtown streets were bustling with shoppers. "Besides," she said, "Grace will be here any minute."

But Elyse wouldn't budge, so Connie refilled their iced tea glasses while Emma chatted away.

Within a half-hour, both Grace and the installer from the security company had arrived. The technician brought a new security system that included four cameras and an alarm. He got right to work, saying it would take about four hours to install.

Shortly after the installer began his work, the technician from the glass company also arrived to replace the window, and in no time the store was bustling with activity.

Elyse and Emma left, and Connie caught Grace up to speed on everything that had happened that day, starting with her 6:00 AM wake-up call from Mickey to their discovery of Natasha's envelope in the wall.

"There's never a dull moment with you, is there, honey? I take one morning off and all this happens. I can't imagine what would happen if I ever left you for a week," Grace said.

"Come on. Let's finish getting this jewelry priced. It's the last major task we have to complete before Saturday," Connie said.

They worked hard for the rest of the day while Ginger mostly napped in her bed, occasionally lifting her head, apparently to make sure she wasn't missing anything.

By mid-afternoon, the window was replaced. The alarm system installer finished up earlier than expected and gave the women a tutorial on operating the system, including the computer software that stored the video footage. Connie even had remote access to the system from her phone.

After patiently answering all their questions, the installer left. One more major task was checked off her to-do list.

Just as they were about finished pricing all the merchandise, Connie's cell phone rang. Her heart sank when she saw that it was Gianna. She completely forgot that she had promised to call on Sunday to say hello to the twins. With everything that happened that night, it had slipped her mind.

"Hey, sis. I'm so sorry I forgot to call you. I had a weekend you wouldn't believe."

"I figured something was up. It's not like you to forget to call when you said you would."

After talking for a few minutes with the twins, Gianna took back the phone. Even with their limited conversation skills, it did Connie a world of good to hear their tiny voices.

"So, what's been going on? I got a little worried when I realized it was Tuesday, and you still hadn't called."

Connie explained about her date with Zach, finding Natasha's body, and the break-in to her store. She couldn't help but laugh when the first thing Gianna picked up on was her date with Zach.

"Wait, so you went on a first date with a cop and on that date, you discovered a dead body?"

"When you put it that way, it sounds exciting. Technically it was a skeleton, and it was actually kind of heart-wrenching."

"Are you kidding me? That's the best first date *ever*. If you two end up together, you'll be telling the story for the rest of your lives. Heck, I'm going to be telling this story for the rest of *my* life. It's just another way I can live vicariously through you."

Connie smiled. Her sister had a way of making her feel better, no matter what the circumstances.

"By the way, that doesn't mean I'm not terrified by the rest of what you told me. I hope your new boyfriend is keeping a close eye on you."

"They are all taking good care of me here. I've made some great new friends. I can't wait for you to meet them the next time you come down. And Grace, of course, has been awesome."

"I'm thrilled she is working with you in the shop. Auntie Concetta would love that."

Connie smiled at her sister across fifteen-hundred miles.

"I know. I think of that all the time. Grace is actually here today. We're pricing jewelry, and I had a security system installed. Don't worry. I'm in good hands."

Connie walked back into the store and handed Grace the phone. "Someone wants to say 'hi'."

Grace's face lit up when she heard Gianna's voice.

Connie smiled at the friendly conversation that took place between the two of them.

Before handing Connie back the phone, she heard Grace say, "I promise I'll watch out for her. But your sister has a mind of her own." Grace shot Connie a stern look. "There's only so much I can do."

# Chapter 17

LATE WEDNESDAY MORNING, after enjoying a leisurely paddle down the beach on her new board, Connie headed to the shop. She opened the sunroof of her silver Jetta as she and Ginger cruised down the boulevard to *Just Jewelry*. The sun was hot as it beat down into the car, but Connie couldn't resist the fresh air.

The shelves were stocked and the jewelry was priced, so all that remained before the grand opening were some last-minute preparations and a few items on the punch list for Steve or Brittany. Connie had texted Steve, and he assured her someone would be by before Saturday.

It was her goal to have all the tasks complete by the end of the day on Thursday, which would leave

Friday free for last-minute or unexpected tasks. Even with Grace having the day off and the extra work from the break-in, it looked like she would finish a full day ahead of schedule.

After a couple of hours of cleaning, Connie looked around with satisfaction and settled into the sofa to people-watch through the front window. Shoppers, laden with shopping bags, perused display windows, while others strolled down the sidewalks, looking as if they had no particular destination or care in the world. Sunburned beachgoers, with coolers and beach chairs in tow, strolled to and from the beach.

While Connie observed passersby through her display window, gray clouds suddenly rolled in, and the sky grew darker. People began picking up their pace as they came in off the beach and headed quickly toward their cars. Some were opting to head into Gallagher's for a bite to eat while they waited for the sun to return.

Connie had to laugh when she saw Ginger watching like a little person from next to her on the sofa, as if she owned the shop. "I guess a rainstorm has its benefits," Connie said. "People are coming in off the beach and heading into restaurants and shops."

Just as the words came out of her mouth, she heard the roar of thunder, and the skies opened. Within a few minutes, raindrops were bouncing off the sidewalks at a pretty good clip. The passersby increased both in number and speed, and amidst the approaching crowd was Gallagher with his t-shirt pulled over his head. Connie jumped up and tapped on the window, motioning for him to take shelter in her shop.

By the time he made it into the store, he was dripping wet. Connie held up her index finger. "Don't move." She disappeared into the back room and returned, tossing him one of the dry towels she had stored out back for emergencies such as these.

"I was on my favorite bench enjoying a smoothie when the skies opened up," he said.

Connie laughed. "The good news is the temperature's in the eighties, not in the forties like in Boston. It's one thing to be wet, but quite another to be *cold* and wet."

Gallagher mock-shivered. "Way to look on the bright side, I guess."

Connie was just about to offer him a warm beverage when the door opened again, and to Connie's surprise, Tracy walked in. When Connie introduced Gallagher and Tracy, Gallagher studied her as if trying to place her.

"You don't want this thing to get waterlogged," she said, taking Tracy's dripping wet phone and placing it on the table. Then she went back to the storage room to throw Gallagher's wet towel in a laundry bag and fetch a clean one for Tracy and a smaller one to wrap around the phone.

Tracy gave the store a thorough once-over while drying off. "I was in town picking up a sandwich for dinner and thought I'd stop by to see the store and ask if you had given any more thought to your accounting needs."

"I appreciate your stopping by," Connie said. "Unfortunately, I haven't had time to think about it." Connie distinctly remembered telling Tracy that she wouldn't be hiring anyone until things got up and running. Either Tracy was a persistent businesswoman, or she had another motive for coming by.

Tracy squirmed under Gallagher's searching gaze. "I'd better go," she said, looking anxiously around the store. "My dinner is waiting for me."

Connie handed her a flyer for the grand opening, asking her to spread the word, and Tracy was out the door.

A ping coming from Tracy's phone alerted Connie to the fact that she had left it behind. She took it from the towel, about to run out to try to catch her when she noticed who the text was from. Her jaw dropped as she held up the phone for Gallagher to see.

"What? Why is she receiving a text from Jordan Sugrue?" he asked.

Connie started to read the message aloud. "*Meet me in a half hour in the park. I want to know...* That's all that's visible on the lock screen. I can't read the rest of it without her password."

Connie pointed to a gray Nissan parked out front. "That's your car, isn't it?"

Gallagher nodded that it was.

"I'll bring Tracy the phone and meet you in your car. We can follow her to see what they're up to."

Ginger looked content chewing on a rawhide bone in her doggie bed, so Connie opted to let her be. It would be the first time she ever left her alone in the store, so she said a quick prayer that both her store and her dog would be okay.

Connie caught up with Tracy before she got into her car and returned the phone. While Tracy was looking down at her phone, apparently reading Jordan's text, Connie slipped into Gallagher's car.

"There was no sandwich in Tracy's car. I looked for it as I was handing her the phone."

While they followed Tracy through town and into the parking lot of the Sapphire Beach State Park, the rain stopped almost as quickly as it had started. Gallagher parked the car a safe distance from Tracy, and they watched her as she kept a nervous eye on the entrance.

Connie was at the park for the second time in one week. She had been meaning to visit ever since she got back to Sapphire Beach, but this wasn't what she had in mind.

"You stay here," she said to Gallagher, with her hand on the door handle. "If Jordan sees you, he'll recognize you."

Gallagher grabbed her arm. "And if Tracy sees you, she'll recognize *you*. You can't go out there."

"How are we going to hear them?" she asked. As they were talking, a black Mercedes pulled into the parking lot.

"That's him," Gallagher said. "We'll just have to see what we can learn from their body language."

"Please tell me Jordan doesn't know your car," Connie said.

"We're safe. I only bought this car last year."

Jordan exited his Mercedes and approached Tracy. Even from a distance her agitation was evident. They spoke for a few minutes, and Jordan went back to his car. He opened the passenger door and pulled out a styrofoam cup, then glanced around the parking lot.

Connie and Gallagher dropped down as fast as they could. The closest trash receptacle was right next to where they were parked.

"He's coming this way," Connie said. She held her breath as his footsteps approached the car. He paused for a few seconds, and the only sound Connie could hear was blood pumping through her veins. She tried to push aside her fear and think of a plan in case their cover was blown.

Luckily, she didn't need one. She and Gallagher both let out a long sigh of relief when the sound of his footsteps indicated he was heading in the other direction.

"We almost ended up buried in the park like Natasha," Gallagher whispered. "Let's stay down until he pulls out."

They waited a couple of minutes after hearing Jordan's car start, then they sat up. Connie felt as though her heart stopped when she looked out the passenger window and saw Tracy standing there with her hands on her hips, looking down into the car.

Connie's heart jump-started for the second time in five minutes.

They exited the car in haste and surrounded Tracy.

"Why are you associated with Jordan Sugrue?" Connie asked. "Are you connected with Natasha's murder?"

Tracy remained silent.

"That's all right. You don't have to say anything. We're going to the police," Gallagher said.

Suddenly Tracy's expression turned to fear. "Wait, please don't do that!" she cried. "I didn't touch Natasha."

"But you were skimming off the top of her business," Connie said. "Was Jordan in on it with you?"

"It's not what you think."

Connie opened the car door. "Let's go, Gallagher. We have a stop to make at the police station."

Tracy put her hands on her face and began to sob. "Please don't. I'm begging you. They'll kill her for sure."

Connie had started to get into the car, but Gallagher motioned for her to hold up. "Where do I know you from?" Gallagher asked.

"You have to swear that you won't tell a soul if I tell you. My little sister's life depends on it." Tracy was begging.

"Who is your sister?" Gallagher asked.

"Tiffany," Tracy said. "Tiffany Peterson."

Gallagher let out a long breath and leaned against his car. "She's a member of New Light," he said to Connie.

"That's right," Tracy said. "When Jordan found out I was Natasha's accountant and Tiffany's sister, he started blackmailing me. He said if I didn't see to it that her business failed, he would kill my sister."

"So that's when you started stealing from *Natasha's Boutique*?"

"It was the only way I could ensure Tiffany's safety. Jordan thought that if Natasha's business failed, she would be forced return to him. I didn't want to do it, I swear. But my sister's life depended on it."

"What were you looking for in my shop today?" Connie asked. "I saw you looking around, and I know you didn't come by to ask me about my accounting needs."

Tears threatened to spill from Tracy's eyes again. "Natasha had some type of evidence against Jordan, and he wanted to get his hands on it. He said if I could find it, he would let Tiffany go free, once and for all."

"So, it was you who broke into my shop early Tuesday morning?"

"What? No, it wasn't me, I swear. If I broke in at night and couldn't find anything, why would I go by during the day while you were there? Jordan knows that your grand opening is Saturday, so he told me to go by and see if I could locate any potential hiding places before the store got busy with customers. It was a long shot, but I told him I'd try."

"If you didn't break into my store, do you know who did?"

"I have no idea. If it was Jordan and he couldn't find anything when he broke in, I doubt he would have sent me this afternoon to poke around."

Tracy looked nervously around the parking lot. "I have to go. If Jordan should come back for any reason and he sees me talking to you, my sister's life will be over."

Tracy's shoulders were hanging low as she took a few steps toward her car. She stumbled but was able to catch her balance.

Connie ran up beside her and supported her with her arm, afraid she was going to collapse, and Gallagher stood behind her, ready to catch her if she did.

Tracy seemed to regain her strength and continued on. Then she turned and faced Connie and Gallagher. "If you guys can do anything to bring down Sugrue, you would be an answer to prayer. I'm terrified for my sister. He's almost finished building a compound on some land that he inherited from his parents. I have a feeling that, once New Light members move there, things are going to get worse fast."

# Chapter 18

CONNIE AND GALLAGHER drove back downtown in silence. Connie's mind was whirling, and judging from Gallagher's intense expression, he, too, was trying to wrap his mind around what they had just learned.

Since there were no parking spaces available on their street, Gallagher pulled his Nissan into a lot a couple of blocks from *Just Jewelry*. Many local business owners and employees, including Connie, parked there, since they offered a discounted monthly pass to downtown workers.

As they walked back, Gallagher broke his pensive silence. "I didn't want to say anything in front of Tracy, but once she told me who Tiffany was, I remembered some things about her. She was just getting into New Light as Natasha and I were planning our exit strategy, but I remember that she was pretty into it. She bought everything Sugrue dished out - hook, line, and sinker."

Connie's heart tightened as she thought of her own sister. "Poor Tracy. I can't imagine being in the position of having to do something unethical to save my sister's life. I can't imagine a worse predicament."

Gallagher stared at the sidewalk pavement as they continued walking. "Knowing Sugrue, I'm not surprised. Now that you've seen his true colors, maybe you can understand why Natasha didn't want him anywhere near Victoria."

"Do you think Tracy will tell him that we followed her?"

"It's in Tiffany's best interest that he doesn't know, so she won't say anything."

All Connie could do was hope that he was right. She was never so glad to live in a secure building like Palm Paradise. But just the same, she would be extra sure to keep her door locked.

When they arrived back at *Just Jewelry*, Connie invited Gallagher inside, but he declined. "I'd better get in there to help out," he said, pointing to the steady stream of customers heading into his restaurant. "But you have my number. Text or call if you need anything."

She flashed him a grateful smile. "The same goes for you, Gallagher."

Both Ginger and the store had survived the dog's first solo stay in the shop, so Connie decided to quit while she was ahead and call it a day. She had only worked for a couple of hours that day, but the store was in great shape for the grand opening. It wouldn't hurt to conserve her strength for the hectic days ahead. Besides, her encounter with Tracy had dampened her mood, and she felt like doing something that might clear her head.

When she got back to Palm Paradise, she took Ginger for a stroll along the boulevard, then dropped her off at the condo so she could continue her walk along the shoreline. Connie could have taken Ginger, but she didn't feel like giving her the bath she would certainly need after playing on the beach.

The silky sand pressing between her toes and the scent of salty air did wonders for her spirit as she made her way along the beach. She walked on the hard sand where she could feel the rhythmic crashing of the waves over her feet. It was about 5:00, and there were still children playing in the water while sunbathers absorbed the weaker rays of the day. In a surge of ambition, Connie resolved to walk out to the pier, a mile from her condo.

As she got closer, she noticed Mickey Miranda sitting next to the giant wooden structure with his knees pulled to his chest, gazing out at the water. His melancholy expression matched her mood. Not wanting to startle him, she approached him in silence and sat down a few feet away. It took some time for him to realize she was there.

"Connie, I didn't see you. What brings you down here this time of day?" he asked, finally noticing her. He gave her a half-smile, then continued staring toward the horizon.

She allowed her gaze to drift outward over the Gulf in the same direction as Mickey's. "I guess I just came out for a walk to think. I know I never met her, but I just can't get Natasha's murder off my mind."

She turned to face him and saw that his eyes had filled with tears.

"I just feel so guilty. That young woman was murdered, and all I did was give her grief about the rent." He pulled his knees closer to his body. "I really believed that she was doing drugs. But when I saw your shop broken into, and it was evident that the intruder was looking for something specific, it became clear to me that someone had been harassing Natasha, too. Who knows? Maybe she would still be here if I had given her the benefit of the doubt and dug a little deeper into Jordan Sugrue's accusations."

Connie cringed when she realized that Mickey would probably feel even worse when he learned that Tracy was stealing from her. But at least it appeared as though her landlord wasn't a killer. That was something positive.

"You couldn't have known all that, Mickey. Besides, whatever problems Natasha had, they predated her arrival at Sapphire Beach."

"I did an online search for Jordan Sugrue on Tuesday after the break-in. I've been kicking myself, because I should have done that a long time ago. What I found was disturbing."

Connie nodded. "I did the same thing. He's bad news."

"I can't shake from my mind that smug look on his face. He seemed more normal when he came to talk to me last year about his suspicions about Natasha. I truly believed he was just a concerned father watching out for his daughter."

Connie hated to think of him having custody of Victoria, but she didn't say anything, because she didn't want to make Mickey feel worse.

"Did you see the look on the faces of his 'disciples' as he spewed his poison?"

Connie nodded. "It was hard to watch."

"I couldn't help but get sucked into a few of the videos that the community posted this week. They were all gathered with him for several days at some retreat center in Colorado listening to him spout his nonsense. It made me sick just listening to the things he said."

"Let's hope the police will be able to stop him," Connie said.

"Just promise me you'll be careful, Connie. He was obviously looking for something in your shop."

"Wait, Mickey. Do you remember how long that retreat in Colorado was?"

"The New Light website said they were there from Friday until last night."

"If that's true, that means he probably couldn't have broken into my shop."

Tracy had said that she thought it was unlikely that it was Jordan, but this news seemed to provide more confirmation that it hadn't been him.

Mickey jumped up. "Oh my gosh, you're right. One of the talks was Monday night, so unless he flew, he wouldn't have had time to get back to Sapphire Beach later that night. I have to tell the police in case they don't know. They can check the flight manifests and find out for sure."

Mickey ran off, stumbling across the sand, without bothering to say goodbye.

She shook her head, smiled at the comical sight, and made her way back to Palm Paradise. The sun was setting, and she was ready to call it a night.

Even after walking back home, Connie was still wound up from her conversation with Mickey, and it was too early for bed. She pulled out Natasha's journal, hoping to find some indication of who else, besides Jordan, could have had it in for Natasha.

She wasn't ruling him out as the killer just because he likely hadn't been the one to break into her store, especially since she no longer suspected Mickey and

Tracy. Even though he was likely in Colorado during the break-in, he could have been collaborating with somebody.

She didn't have much luck with the diary. It was more about Natasha's own hopes and dreams for herself and her daughter and didn't dwell too much on the past. Besides 'Mac', who turned out to be Gallagher, she didn't reveal any names from her past life.

Frustrated, she tossed it aside and instead got to work on the necklace she was hoping to complete before Saturday. Working with her hands always helped her to think, and it was better than sitting passively on the couch. At least she was being productive while she reflected.

Whoever broke into *Just Jewelry* was clearly searching for something, most likely the evidence Emma had inadvertently discovered behind the wall with her volleyball. If that's the case, since Jordan *couldn't* have broken into the shop, then the intruder had to be somehow connected with Jordan. Why else would he or she be trying to get hold of the evidence that Natasha had against him?

The other option was that the killer and the intruder were not connected at all. Perhaps somebody affiliated with New Light broke into Connie's store to find the photos, audio files, and key, but Natasha's death didn't have anything to do with that person.

Connie was so absorbed in thought that, before she knew it, the necklace was complete. She looked it over, pleased with her work, and set it aside to take to the store the next day.

With her task complete, she opened her laptop and pulled up some images and videos from New Light. Jordan had so many adoring fans, so anyone who wanted to please him could be involved. As she scanned the photos, she couldn't take her eyes off the sea of faces that seemed to hang on his every word.

Connie looked again at the two women who seemed so familiar and tried to place them. She studied both faces - first one, then the other, until she finally realized that one of them was Tiffany Peterson. Connie had recognized her from the photo that she saw in Tracy's foyer when she paid her a visit a couple of weeks ago.

That explained who one of the women was, but she still couldn't place the second one, who was standing next to Tiffany. She scrutinized her face for a long time but to no avail. The answer stayed buried just beneath her consciousness.

Eventually she gave up, hoping it might come to her if she put it aside.

"I wish I knew what the key from the envelope unlocked," Connie said to Ginger, who was resting contentedly by her feet. "Perhaps that would answer some of these questions."

# Chapter 19

THURSDAY WHIZZED BY in a blurry haze. In the morning, Connie and Grace worked hard taking care of last-minute details for the grand opening, and when Connie was finally able to convince Grace to go home and save her energy for the long weekend ahead, she spent the rest of afternoon creating some simple jewelry pieces and posting on social media to hype up the event on Saturday.

On Friday, Connie arrived at the shop mid-morning, unlocked the door, and punched in the passcode to disengage the new alarm system. Ginger made a beeline to her new chew toy by her bed in the back of the store, and as she disappeared behind the counter, Connie heard footsteps growing quicker and louder on the pavement outside the shop.

She positioned her keys in her hand, preparing to use them as a weapon if need be, pulled the door tight behind her, and locked it. Just as she was ready to turn the alarm back on, Zach's confused face appeared, peering in through the window. He was holding a bouquet of sunflowers.

Connie quickly opened the door, laughing at the misunderstanding. "I'm so sorry, Zach," she said, stepping aside and motioning for him to come in. "I guess I'm a little on edge between the break-in and my big day tomorrow."

"No worries," he said. "The last thing I wanted to do was scare you, but I'm glad to see you're being aware of your surroundings."

"I'm trying, although I should have realized that robbers don't usually come with flowers," Connie said, smiling as she accepted the bouquet.

"I'm on my way into work, but I wanted to stop by to wish you luck with the grand opening tomorrow. I plan to come by, but you'll probably be really busy, so I was hoping to catch you this morning."

"Thank you, Zach. The flowers are beautiful."

While she went out back to grab a vase, Zach explored the store.

"It looks great in here," he said when she returned. "I love that you gave the Fair Trade section such a prime location in the store."

Connie put the sunflowers in a glass cylindrical vase and placed them in the middle of the table. "I'm hoping this endeavor is successful for so many reasons, but a major one is that it could provide some much-needed income for my overseas artisans."

"My money's on you," Zach said.

She wasn't sure if it was his confidence in her or his smile that melted her heart. Maybe a little of both.

Since Zach had to get right to work, Connie walked him to the door. "Are you any closer to knowing who broke into my store on Tuesday?"

"Unfortunately, we don't have any answers for you yet, but we do know it wasn't Sugrue. We were able to confirm that he was indeed in Colorado on Tuesday night, as Mickey suspected. His whereabouts are accounted for during most of the night, and he wasn't listed as a passenger on any of the flight manifests. There is no way he could have been able to get to Florida and back in such a short window of time."

"Unless he sent someone else do his dirty work," Connie suggested.

"We're looking into that possibility. Part of the reason I stopped by was to make sure you are being careful, since we still don't know who broke into your shop. Whoever the intruder is probably doesn't know that you found the envelope, so be extra careful," Zach said. "I know you installed the alarm system, but you might be better off not being here alone, especially at night, until we catch the person."

That would make things difficult for Connie since, aside from Grace working part-time, she was the only person to work the shop. She was planning to hire another employee when things got off the ground, but she didn't know how long that would take.

"Do you think the same person who killed Natasha broke into my shop?"

"I shouldn't tell you this, but that's another reason you need to be extra vigilant. Jordan also has a solid alibi for the night Natasha was killed, so he is no longer a suspect in her murder."

"He still could have had one of his people do it."

"That's true, but we're leaning away from him. The local sheriff is keeping a close eye on him for other things, but we don't think he is responsible for Natasha's death. At least not directly."

"What about the key we found?" Connie asked. "Do you know what it belongs to?"

"We think it opens a safety deposit box. We'll be checking on some possible locations today."

Connie took a step closer to Zach. "Thanks for letting me know. I appreciate your having my back."

He took her hand and gently squeezed it.

"You can thank me by staying safe."

After Zach left, Ginger wandered to the front of the store, apparently tired of her chew toy.

"Looks like we're back at square one," Connie said. Ginger looked up with her button eyes and seemed to agree.

It was a good thing that Connie already had things ready to go for the grand opening, because about a half hour after Zach left, Elyse came in.

Connie was thrilled to see her friend.

"I thought you might be nervous about tomorrow, even though I know you're going to crush it. I figured I'd stop by to see how you're doing."

"It turns out I'm ahead of schedule," Connie said. "Would you like to get an ice cream? We can take Ginger and eat it on a bench by the water."

Elyse's face lit up. "Sounds perfect."

The two women made their way down the street to *Friendly Scoops*. "Remind me to thank Zach for sending you here," Connie said with a smirk. "I'll bet you the necklace I just finished making that he sent you over, so I wouldn't be alone."

Elyse laughed. "You got us. He texted me to let me know you could use some company. He said you seemed a little on edge when he stopped by earlier."

"He was right. But it's nothing a cup of rum raisin with my BFF can't fix," Connie said, looping her arm through Elyse's.

Elyse opted for the rocky road, and since the sun was gaining strength, Connie asked for a cup of water for Ginger, as well. Then they settled in on an empty bench under the shade of a palm tree.

A young woman pushing a stroller stopped in front of them, just long enough to adjust the sunshade over her baby before continuing on her way.

Elyse's eyes followed the stroller until it disappeared behind some people halfway down the pier.

"I've been thinking about what you shared last week," Connie said. "About not being able to have any more children."

"It makes me sad sometimes. Josh and I have so much love we could offer another child, and Emma would be such a great big sister."

"I know what you mean," Connie said. "I'm thirty-four years old and not even in a relationship, so it's likely that I won't have any children. It seems the older I get, the more I think about it."

"What about Zach? You never know what could happen there."

"He's a great guy, and I'm looking forward to seeing him again, but we barely know each other. What I'm getting at is, even without having children, there are a lot of ways to be a mother. If I had a family, there is no way I could have devoted as much time as I have to *Feeding the Hungry*. I like to think my work helps make life better for children I will never even meet."

Elyse put her hand on Connie's forearm. "There's not a doubt in my mind that that's true for you. My work is fulfilling in its own way, but not like yours."

"I'm just saying that there is a reason for every desire in our hearts. Trust in that, and be open to what Providence might bring your way. That's all."

Connie looked down at Ginger's pleading eyes.

"She's waiting to hear what you'll say next," Elyse said, laughing.

"She's waiting for my ice cream to fall is more like it," Connie said, as she stroked the silky fur on the top of the dog's head. "I'm sorry, sweetie, but this kind isn't good for you."

"Speaking of what's good for you," Elyse said, pulling her phone from her purse to check the time. "I'd better get back to work. I have a showing in twenty minutes."

Connie walked Elyse back to her car, and she and Ginger returned to work.

Connie double-checked her completed checklist. Confirm the delivery of appetizers. Check. Purchase beverages. Check. Assemble gift bags containing jewelry to be given away as door prizes. Check. Prepare posts for social media. Check.

The one thing she hadn't counted on in her plan to have everything ready early was that she would have nothing to do but worry the day before the big event. All that was left was some final cleaning so everything would sparkle for the big day. She might even be able to leave early.

When Brittany entered the store an hour later, with her toolbox in hand, Connie was grateful for the distraction. It had slipped her mind that she might be coming this afternoon to finish up the last few items on the punch list.

"I hope this is still a good time," Brittany said. "I wanted to come yesterday, but Steve has had me running all over the place."

Connie jumped up and greeted her with more enthusiasm than the situation warranted. She was glad for the company. "No problem at all. I'm just sitting here waiting for tomorrow to arrive."

Brittany scanned the store. "Well, it looks amazing in here. I'm sure you'll be a huge success. I'll start patching the drywall out back," she said, and disappeared into the storeroom.

While Connie waited, her thoughts once again wandered over to Natasha. Since everyone she suspected had been cleared, she was at a loss. She brought her computer over to the table and pulled up some of the videos of Jordan Sugrue.

She clicked on a few different links. The more she looked at them, the more she realized that there seemed to be the same core group always in the first row at his events. She looked at the faces one by one before settling once again on the woman standing next to Tracy. Where had Connie seen her before?

Connie once again searched her mind but came up blank. As she studied the images, she could hear Brittany in the store room pulling the large shelving unit away from the wall, then cutting out the loose drywall around the hole, and then, a few minutes later, the sound of a metal tool spreading joint compound over the patched area of the wall. Since her nerves were a little on edge over the grand opening tomorrow, she found she was agitated by the noise, even though it wouldn't normally bother her. Finally, it was quiet, and she could think again.

She stared at a photo with the familiar-looking woman front and center. She enlarged it on her computer screen. *Wait a minute.*

She pulled up some photos of Jordan speaking earlier that week in Colorado and searched the front row, but there was no sign of the woman.

Because she was in Sapphire Beach, breaking into Connie's store.

Suddenly the pieces came together in her mind, and Connie's mouth went as dry as the sand on Sapphire Beach.

Connie hadn't told Steve or Brittany about the hole in the drywall out back, and Brittany hadn't been in the shop after the break-in, so how did she know about the hole in the wall?

She studied the woman in the photo on her computer screen again. Her hair was dark brown in the photo, and Connie knew her as a blond, but it was definitely her.

Connie was alone in the shop with the killer.

# Chapter 20

CONNIE BLASTED OUT a quick text to Gallagher. *I know who the killer is.*

Then she glanced up at the door and started to stand. If she could casually make it out of the store, she would be able to call the police.

Suddenly a chill ran down her body as she realized she could no longer hear Brittany repairing the wall in the next room. Why had the store grown silent? *Hopefully she's just taking a break,* Connie thought. But the feeling in the pit of her stomach telling her that she was no longer alone in the room grew stronger with each heartbeat.

Realizing she still had her cell phone in hand, Connie quickly navigated to the voice memo feature in her phone and began recording. Then she discreetly slipped it into her pocket as a precaution in case she couldn't make it to the door.

She was about to bolt when a dusty hand pressed itself hard against her mouth and her computer, sitting on the table in front of her with Brittany's photo expanded on the screen, was slammed shut.

Connie tried to react with something from her self-defense training, but it was too late. Brittany had grabbed her from behind and forced her into a tight headlock.

She looked out the windows in vain for a passerby who might be witnessing the scene and calling the police, but there was nobody in sight. Connie's airways tightened from the headlock, and she had no choice but to let herself be pulled out back, where Brittany proceeded to force her onto a folding chair in the back room. She grabbed a piece of rope from her toolbox with her free hand and pushed Connie onto a folding chair.

Knowing she was going to be tied up, Connie put her hands together in front of her body and offered them to Brittany. Having her hands tied in front of her body rather than behind her would at least give her a fighting chance at escaping.

As Brittany was binding her hands, Connie remembered another trick she learned in the self-defense classes that her parents insisted she take before moving to Africa. She discreetly rotated one of her hands until it was at a 45-degree angle to create a gap between her wrists. This would give her more space work with if she could find the right opportunity to try to break free. She also twisted her body from side to side to make it harder for Brittany to make a good knot.

"You're a member of New Light," Connie said as Brittany struggled to secure her hands. Brittany's obsession with self-empowerment made more sense now.

"I'm more than just a member."

"Let me guess. Jordan Sugrue is the boyfriend you're moving home to be with, now that the compound is nearly built. Did you kill Natasha out of jealousy?"

While Connie had been twisting her body, she caught a glimpse of her spare jewelry-making tool kit on the shelf several feet away. If only she could get her hands on one of those sharp tools. Her thoughts were interrupted when Brittany pulled out a gun from her toolbox and pointed it at Connie.

"Natasha never appreciated Jordan. She would have destroyed him if she could. She even blackmailed him into letting her leave the community. I wasn't going to allow her to get away with that and to use the information she had to send Jordan to prison for life and destroy New Light."

The photos and audio files that Connie had found in the wall wouldn't send Jordan to prison for life. She wished she knew what the key was all about.

"Natasha just wanted to start over in Sapphire Beach. He could have just let her go," Connie said.

"He *did* let her go. But Natasha refused to turn over the evidence she had against him, even when Jordan promised to leave her alone. I couldn't take the chance that she would turn it over to the police and ruin everything. I had to get rid of Natasha for the sake of everyone in New Light. I wanted to prove to Jordan that I was worthy of the community's respect and of being his future wife."

Connie hoped the device was still recording from inside her pocket.

"Jordan is a prophet," Brittany continued. "Not everyone understands him or what it takes to be a leader. Victoria is better off with him. And with me."

Connie's stomach turned at the thought of Brittany and Jordan raising Victoria.

"Jordan didn't tell you to kill Natasha, did he? You did that all on your own."

Brittany sneered. "He said to just leave her be, but I wasn't going to stand by and take the chance that she would ruin his life and mine. Not with the dirt she had on him."

Apparently, catching on that something wasn't right, Ginger started barking at Brittany. She grabbed her and then kicked the whimpering dog out the back door.

Fear shot through Connie's body as she imagined Ginger wandering onto the busy street out front and getting hit by a car.

She swallowed her fear, and while Brittany was pushing Ginger out the back door, she made a dash for the awl, one of the sharpest tools in her jewelry-making tool kit. She held it by the handle and concealed the pointed end with her forearm.

"Steve is going to know that you were with me," Connie said, trying to pretend there wasn't a gun pointed at her so she could think straight.

"Not if I tell him nobody was here when I came by. Okay, enough talking. We're going for a ride."

With a gun pointed at her head, Connie had no choice but to follow.

"Hurry up!" Brittany said, jabbing the gun into her back.

A mixture of adrenaline and fear pumped through Connie's veins. Stalling Brittany would be her best shot at escaping.

"So, you're just giving up on finding the evidence that Natasha had against Jordan? If you don't find it, the police still might be able to locate it, and then you and Jordan will lose everything."

"I've searched everywhere, and there's nothing anywhere in this store. If I haven't been able to find it, the police won't, either."

"Maybe the problem is that you don't know where to look. There are a lot of nooks and crannies in this old shop. Did you check the floorboards under this shelf?"

"You're stalling," Brittany said.

"It's where I found some photos that belonged to Natasha," she said, hoping her lie sounded believable.

"What photos?" Brittany slid her foot under the shelf to feel for the loose board.

Seeing that Brittany was slightly off balance, with one foot partially under the shelf, Connie slammed Brittany's hands, gun and all, onto the shelf with her elbow, then jabbed the sharp tool as hard as she could with her hands bound, into the top of Brittany's hand.

Brittany let out a high-pitched squeal from the pain and had no choice but to release her grip on the gun. Connie grabbed it and cut her hands free with a pair of pliers in her jewelry-making tool kit as Brittany pulled the sharp awl out of her hand. Then Connie backed up a few steps so Brittany wouldn't get any ideas.

Once she was sure she was safe, she then threw Brittany a towel to wrap her hand so blood wouldn't drip on her newly refinished floors.

Connie forced Brittany toward the front of the store and over to the table. It felt safer there, since the table was in view of the front door and the windows.

She pulled her phone out of her pocket and just as she was dialing 911, she heard sirens approaching. Two police cars pulled up in front of the store, and two police officers burst through the door. Sapphire Beach Fire Rescue and Collier County EMS arrived next.

Finally, Gallagher came in behind them, holding a trembling Ginger against his chest.

# Chapter 21

CONNIE PASSED BRITTANY'S gun to one of the deputies just as Zach and Josh arrived.

Then, trembling almost as much as Ginger, she took the dog from Gallagher's arms and held her close as she explained everything that happened, starting from the moment Brittany came into the shop to complete the punch list.

Brittany objected to Connie's story and accused her of making it all up until, remembering her attempt to record what had just taken place, Connie pulled her phone out of her pocket and played the audio file that revealed the truth. She had gotten everything.

She promptly texted the file to Zach and Josh and emailed it to herself for safekeeping. She wanted to be absolutely certain there would be no chance of losing it.

As Brittany was being escorted away, Grace wandered into the store, her jaw hanging low as she tried to make sense of the scene she walked into.

"I just came by to make sure you weren't bored, since there wasn't much work left for you to do today, but I can see that's not the case."

Connie caught Grace up to speed, and Gallagher added his side. When Connie's text came through, revealing that she had figured out who the killer was, he was talking to a customer, so he didn't see it for a few minutes. When he noticed the message, he started to go over to talk to Connie, but before he could get very far, Ginger wandered into the street. There were cars coming from both directions, so he stepped out to stop the traffic, and when he picked her up, she was shaking, so he knew something was wrong. He immediately called 911.

Zach chimed in. "We didn't know that Brittany was the killer, but we did learn something important earlier this afternoon," he said. "We discovered that the key you found in the envelope in the wall belonged to a safety deposit box at Blue Waters

Bank. We went there a couple of hours ago, and it contained evidence that proved that Jordan Sugrue was responsible for intentionally setting a fire that killed his parents."

Gallagher pulled out one of the chairs from the table and sat down. He let out a deep breath. "I've known for a long time that the guy's a monster, and I've seen him sink to some pretty low depths," he said. "But this news surprises even me."

"Natasha managed to get her hands on some incriminating evidence, so he'll be going away for a long time," Zach said.

"After all that, in the end, Natasha's death had nothing to do with Sugrue," Connie said.

Zach shook his head. "No, not directly. In fact, he was better off when Natasha was alive, because as long as he left her and their daughter alone, he wouldn't have to worry about the evidence getting out. He must have panicked when she disappeared, since he didn't know where she hid everything. He knew that if somebody stumbled across it, it would be all be over for him."

"So, it wasn't just that he was worried about his reputation and status as leader of New Light,"

Connie said, "but that he stood to spend the rest of his life in prison if the information got out. That's why he was obsessed with finding it."

"Exactly," Zach said.

"Wow," Gallagher said. "I can't believe Natasha never told me about that."

Connie put her hand on his shoulder. "She probably wanted to protect you. She needed your help to get the photos and audio recordings, but she probably figured there was no need for you to know about his role in his parents' death. Ultimately that's the piece of evidence that got her killed, even though the killer was Brittany and not Jordan."

After everything settled down, Connie and Gallagher drove over to the police station to fill out an official statement. Grace took Ginger back to Palm Paradise with her, promising to bring her for a good, long walk, and to have a home-cooked meal waiting for Connie when she returned.

Connie finally returned home at 6:30. She took a hot shower, then called Grace, who brought over a chicken pot pie, Connie's favorite comfort food, which they enjoyed on the balcony with a glass of Chardonnay. The vast ocean that stretched to the horizon did wonders for Connie's nerves. Grace left early so they could both get a good night's sleep before the grand opening.

***

The grand opening was scheduled to take place from noon to 4:00 PM, but Connie and Grace were there bright and early making sure that no detail was overlooked. They performed a last-minute cleaning so the store would sparkle, which Connie had anticipated doing the day before, but was unable to complete with everything that took place. Then they set out gift bags with door prizes - mostly earrings Connie made - put out beverages, and set out plates, napkins, and cups on the oak table. Now all they had to do was wait on the appetizers, which would be delivered just before noon.

Steve had called Connie the night before, apologizing profusely for what happened with Brittany. He was beside himself that he had hired a murderer, and since she was his employee, he felt responsible for what had happened. He even took ten percent off the price of his labor, acknowledging that there was nothing he could do to make it up to Connie, but hoping to express his sincere regret, nonetheless. He also personally finished the punch list that Brittany never completed at 5:00 that morning, so there would be no loose ends for the grand opening.

Connie smiled as she took one last walk through the shop. Everything was just as she hoped it would be. Then she snapped a few more photos and posted them on her social media accounts, in a last-minute effort to drum up some attention. She also texted some photos of the shop to her parents and sister, since they couldn't be there in person.

Grace discovered a powder-blue gift bag with yellow tissue paper behind the circular checkout counter.

"I found one more door prize," she said, bringing it over to the table.

Connie had almost forgotten that she decided to gift Grace with the beautiful necklace that she had been working hard to finish all week.

"This one isn't a door prize. It's for you," she said. "It's just a little something to thank you for all the hard work and extra hours you've put in to help me get ready for today."

Grace gasped as she pulled the necklace from the bag. She absolutely loved the copper-colored satin finish beads and put it right on.

"It means so much to have you here, Grace. You are the closest thing I have to family in Sapphire Beach," she said, pulling her into an affectionate hug. By the time she pulled away, both women's eyes were moist with tears.

A little before noon, Stephanie and Penelope arrived to help out as they had promised. Stephanie took the day off from work, and Gallagher had given Penelope the afternoon off so she could help Connie on her big day. She put them in charge of greeting guests as they came through the door and handing out tickets for door prizes, which would be drawn every half-hour. Connie hoped that, in addition to adding something fun to the day, it would encourage customers to linger. Penelope would also be the official photographer, since she had a talent for taking pictures.

Elyse and Emma arrived at noon with a bouquet of pink roses, just as the caterer was leaving.

"Are you going to tell me what's going on with you?" Connie asked after she put them in a vase and placed them on the coffee table. Elyse had called Connie the night before to tell her that she wouldn't be able to stay long at the grand opening. Connie was disappointed, since Elyse played a huge role in making *Just Jewelry* a reality and in Connie relocating to Sapphire Beach, but the feeling dissipated when she heard the excitement in Elyse's voice. And now the expression of joy on her friend's face had the same affect. She knew it had to be something huge for Elyse to miss out on the festivities of the day.

"Not yet," Elyse said. "I don't want to jinx it, but I promise that Josh, Emma, and I will come by tonight and fill you in on everything."

As they left, the first customers of the day came through the door, and, to Connie's delight, the traffic didn't let up until the end of the day. Her advertising and social media campaign turned out to be a huge success, and customers loved the door prizes.

The Fair Trade merchandise was also well-received. People lingered over the framed pictures and biographies of the artisans, which Connie had placed throughout the Fair Trade section. And with each Fair Trade purchase, Connie included a miniature version of the photo and bio of the artisan who created that particular piece and directed them to the website to learn more about the artisans. Throughout the day, Connie was able to get a wide range of feedback from customers and felt confident in what types of jewelry she would request in her next order.

Fr. Paul Fulton came by as he had promised and chose a bracelet from Kenya as a gift for his sister's birthday. Connie also recognized several other parishioners from Our Lady, Star of the Sea and made a mental note to continue the bulletin ad.

Grace, Stephanie, and Penelope were lifesavers. They took care of many details, such as handing out food and giving away door prize tickets while Grace was busy at the cash register. This left Connie free to socialize with her customers.

Zach came by and brought some friends, but he couldn't stay long, since it turned out he had to cover for Josh, who was with Elyse on their mysterious errand. But she was happy to see him, even if it was just for a little while.

Gertrude also attended. She, too, had no idea what Josh and her great-niece were up to that day, but she brought with her a small crowd of southwest Florida residents, both from Palm Paradise and beyond. Connie was not the least bit surprised to see that Gertrude had such broad influence, but it warmed her heart that she had put it to use promoting *Just Jewelry*.

Although they were busy with their own businesses, Gallagher and Ruby stopped by, followed by Mickey and his wife, Susan. Susan was excited to learn that Connie would be offering jewelry-making classes in the store and joined the mailing list so she could receive all the details.

Mickey looked much better than when Connie had last talked to him under the pier.

"I still feel terrible that I was so quick to believe Jordan and thought the worst about Natasha, but at least now I know that Jordan wasn't the killer," he said. "Brittany would have killed Natasha, anyway. There's nothing I could have done to stop it."

Throughout the day, Connie had had the sensation that she was seeing a parade of her new family in Sapphire Beach march through the store. She was closer to some than others, but the support of every person there meant the world to her.

By the time the last customer left a little after 4:00, Connie couldn't decide if she was more excited at the success of the grand opening or exhausted from having pulled it off. But even after a long afternoon, an ear-to-ear smile lingered on her face.

After her friends helped her clean up, she fed Ginger, who had loved the attention she received throughout the day, and ordered pizza for everyone. Gallagher was also able to get away from the restaurant at that point, so he came back across the street to join them. When they sat at the table to eat, Connie heard a text come through on her phone.

"It's your niece," she said to Gertrude. "She says, 'Stay at the store. We'll be there in a half-hour. We have really big news.'"

# Chapter 22

ZACH RETURNED TO THE STORE before Elyse, Josh, and Emma arrived. "Josh just texted me and told me to meet him here. He said he had some news."

"Yeah, Elyse texted me, too. We're all waiting. Do you have any idea what it could be about?" Connie asked Zach, handing him a paper plate with a slice of pizza.

"I know the local police up in Jordan's area arrested him this morning for his parents' murder, and Josh took a drive up to talk to them about something. But he was all secretive, so I know it wasn't official police business," Zach said.

Connie had been so absorbed in the grand opening that, for the first time all week, she hadn't thought about Natasha, Jordan, or New Light.

"Jordan agreed to plead guilty in order to avoid a death sentence," Zach said. "Although there are no charges against him in relation to Natasha's murder, he did admit to putting the needle in the bushes out back to make it look as though Natasha had a drug problem."

"I'm glad that's cleared up," Connie said. "That will put an end to any rumors floating around that could harm her good name. Now nobody can doubt that she truly did everything possible to give her daughter and herself a fresh start."

Just as everyone was finishing up their pizza, the door chime sounded, and their attention shifted to the front of the store. Walking behind Josh, who entered first, was Emma with her arm wrapped protectively across the shoulders of a little girl, who looked to be about three years old, followed by Elyse.

Elyse bent down and scooped up the child as everyone came over to see what was going on.

The little girl looked around the store, knitting her brow as she studied her surroundings. The child's blond curls framed her round face, and her blue eyes settled on Connie, who had bent over to say hello.

"And who is this little princess?" Connie asked.

"That's Victoria," Penelope said, taking the child into her arms and sobbing. "I never thought I'd see you again."

Victoria smiled, and her reaction showed that she recognized her old friend.

Elyse was beaming with joy. "Josh and I are hoping to adopt Victoria."

Connie felt as though time stopped. She stood in shock as the rest of the group congratulated the new family of four.

"May I?" Connie said to Penelope, holding her arms out toward the child.

Penelope placed Victoria in Connie's arms, and she kissed the child's chubby cheeks.

Josh and Elyse stood next to each other, holding hands.

"When I heard yesterday that Jordan was pleading guilty and that he didn't have any living relatives," Josh said, "I knew Victoria would be put into foster care."

Elyse continued the story where he left off. "Josh and I talked and prayed about it all day and evening, and we decided to move forward. Victoria needs a family, and all three of us have so much love to give, so we decided get the process started."

As Connie held Victoria, Gallagher kissed the child's forehead. "Natasha would be thrilled," he said. "She wanted her daughter to be raised in Sapphire Beach, and if Natasha couldn't raise Victoria herself, she would be so happy to know she found her way to such a beautiful family."

While everyone took turns welcoming Victoria, Connie followed Gallagher to the couch, where he had asked to speak with Josh and Zach.

"What will happen to the members of New Light?" Gallagher asked. "Some of them are in a pretty fragile state."

Josh nodded. "They have been given access to psychological counseling," he said, "but some of them have a long way to go, and the police up there can't force them to accept help."

"If there's anything I can do, please let me know," Gallagher said.

"What about Tiffany Peterson?" Connie asked. "Did you hear anything about her?"

"We notified Tracy after Jordan's arrest, and she immediately drove up to try to convince her sister to come back to Sapphire Beach with her. I had a chance to speak with Tracy while we were up there, and when she learned that Elyse and I wanted to adopt Victoria, she gave me a substantial check. She said that even though she only took money from Natasha's business to save her sister's life, she wanted to make it right. It's rightly Natasha's money, and now Victoria's, so we are going to put it into a savings account for her."

"I'll give you Tracy's phone number," Connie said to Gallagher. "That way you can reach out to her and offer your help for Tiffany."

"I'd like that."

Grace's animated voice came bounding across the store. "Come on, you four. It's time for the Wall of Fame."

"Let's go," Connie said to the others. "She's been waiting for this moment all day."

Penelope had finished printing the photos she took at the grand opening. They would pick out a few of the best and hang them on what Connie and Grace had dubbed the Wall of Fame. The wall, which ran the length of the oak table, would be the *Just Jewelry* family album, visible for everyone to see.

Connie had purchased twenty-five frames of various shapes and sizes that would lend elegance to the collage. The plan was to start with about seven or eight and build as time went on.

Grace had already made a discreet pencil mark to indicate the center of the wall, and it was a given that Concetta's photo would be in the center. Without Concetta leaving the condo to Connie, none of this would have been possible, so with Grace's help, Connie had chosen the perfect picture. Since Concetta had been an actress for most of her adult life, the photo was of her on the set of one of her last movies.

The next to be hung captured Connie with her first friends in Sapphire Beach - Grace, Stephanie, Zach, Elyse, Emma, Josh, and Gertrude. It had been taken at Connie's condo on the night she signed the lease for the shop. Without good friends, this new adventure Connie was embarking on wouldn't be nearly as sweet.

Above that was a picture of Connie's parents, sister, brother-in-law, and twin niece and nephew back in Boston. They would always be a part of everything she did, no matter where Connie found herself.

Then she hung a picture of Natasha, Victoria, Gallagher, and Penelope, because they were a part of the store's history, and Connie hoped the latter three would be part of its future, as well.

Next to that was a picture of Victoria as a toddler in the store, courtesy again of Penelope.

Around those, Connie scattered various pictures from the grand opening, since the store would be non-existent without its customers. Connie was sure to include among them one with Fr. Paul, since one of his homilies helped her to make the decision to open the shop, and one of herself with Gallagher, Penelope, Ruby, and Emily, the owner of *Friendly Scoops*. She knew the support and encouragement of other area business owners would prove to be important, as well.

When the last photo was hung, Connie went out back to the refrigerator and returned with a bottle of champagne and some glasses she had brought for the occasion. She smiled at Zach as she handed him the bottle to do the honors.

While Josh and Gallagher handed out champagne, Connie watched Elyse, beaming with pride at her two girls. It was hard to believe that only three months before, she and Elyse were standing in that same shop, and Elyse was planting the idea in Connie's heart to turn it into a jewelry store.

As Connie reached for her glass, she caught a glimpse of Gallagher's tattoo, and the words of Natasha's diary came flooding back. *He got a tattoo of a majestic eagle to remind himself of how we soared above so many challenges.*

In their own personal way, everyone present was doing just that.

Connie raised her glass. "To new beginnings."

"To new beginnings," they responded heartily.

**The End**

# Next Book in this Series

**Book 3:** *Piers, Pliers and Problems*
Available on Amazon

OR

**Free Prequel:** *Vacations and Victims.*
Meet Concetta and Bethany in the
Sapphire Beach prequel.

Available in ebook or PDF format only at:
BookHip.com/MWHDFP

# Stay in touch!

Join my Readers' Group for periodic updates,
exclusive content, and to be notified of new releases.
Enter your email address at:
BookHip.com/MWHDFP

OR

Email:
angela@angelakryan.com

Facebook:
facebook.com/AngelaKRyanAuthor

Post Office:
Angela K. Ryan, John Paul Publishing, P.O. Box
283, Tewksbury, MA 01876

# ABOUT THE AUTHOR

Angela K. Ryan, author of the *Sapphire Beach Cozy Mystery Series*, writes clean, feel-good stories that uplift and inspire, with mysteries that will keep you guessing.

When she is not writing, Angela enjoys the outdoors, especially kayaking, stand-up paddleboarding, snowshoeing, and skiing. She lives near Boston and loves the change of seasons in New England, but, like her main character, she looks forward to brief escapes to the white, sandy beaches of southwest Florida, where her mother resides.

Angela dreams of one day owning a Cavalier King Charles Spaniel like Ginger, but isn't home enough to take care of one. So, for now, she lives vicariously through her main character, Connie.

Made in the USA
Columbia, SC
24 November 2020